Finding Her Voice

Rose,
Thank you so
much for your
support.
Best
Natalie

Finding Her Voice

Short Stories by Natalie Zellat Dyen

Finding Her Voice

ISBN-13: 978-1-946702-24-1

Published by Freeze Time Media

To all those who discover

what they love to do,

regardless of how old they

are.

Contents

Introduction

Having spent most of my professional life as a technical writer, I expected to explore more "structured" writing projects when I retired, like marketing or grant writing. Then I took a creative writing class and discovered I had a talent for making things up. Who knew?

My writing teacher became my mentor and encouraged me to submit my first story for publication. The good news was that the story was published. The bad news was that the story was published, which led to the false expectation that getting published was easy. After receiving enough rejection slips to paper my powder room, I learned otherwise.

Since that time, seven of my stories, which appear in this collection, have been published in literary journals. Getting published is all well and good, but writing has provided many more intangible benefits that have served me well in my retirement.

First, writing is therapy—only less expensive. Though I can't manage even five minutes of mindful meditation to reduce anxiety and stress, I can spend hours brainstorming characters, plots, beginnings, and endings, and emerge a calmer, saner person on the other side.

Also, writing is empowering. When someone is nasty to me, I can write him into a story and kill him off.

Writing provides me with handy excuses. As an introvert, I find it exhausting to socialize for long periods of time. So, when someone asks me why I'm sitting in a corner by myself staring into space, I tell them I'm working on my next novel. It gets a laugh, and possibly, some respect.

Writing is also an excuse to drink more coffee. Caffeine invariably jump-starts creativity, though sadly, once the caffeine has worn off, and I read what I've written, I'm shocked to discover that I haven't written the great American novel. Which is just an excuse to re-caffeinate.

Finally, writing is a way of processing the difficult or unexpected. Saying "Let it be a writing opportunity" allows me to distance myself from negative events and start the process of turning lemons into lemonade.

One's voice, like one's life, is always a work in progress, and I will continue to enjoy this journey.

When She Could Fly

Afew months before she died, my grandmother taped a picture on her bedroom wall at our beach house. The paper had a ragged edge, as if she'd torn it out of a book. It showed a curly-haired man in a black suit standing on a hilltop, holding hands with a woman who floated above him, wearing a dress the color of grape juice.

"That's Marc Chagall and me," Grandmom told us.

Until that moment, we'd been sure Grandmom's only husband had been Grandpop, and he'd died a long time ago. Each year on her wedding anniversary, Grandmom let down her hair and took her bridal veil and shoes out of a Wanamaker's hatbox. Then the three of us would gather in her bedroom.

"Is my veil on straight, P. J.?" she'd ask my sister, who was clearly her favorite grandchild. "Hand me that mirror." Then she'd slip her feet into white satin pumps. "Look, *kinderlach*, they still fit." If Mom was anywhere nearby, she gave Grandmom a pinched-face look; I don't know if it was the Yiddish or the wedding outfit that got to her.

Sometimes Grandmom asked P. J. to help her with the shoes. "You too, Cookie," she'd add, if she remembered I was there. "Come help me get this one on."

My name isn't really Cookie—it's Ella—but thanks to our mother, we were all called something else, as if our real names were just placeholders. Paula Jean was "P. J." Our older sister, Susan, was "Princess." I think Mom gave us nicknames so we'd be more like the kids at the Baldwin School, a fancy prep school we attended. Kids there were called Muffy, Bitsy, Chip. Our names didn't sound anything like theirs, and I'm sure no one else at school had a grandmother from Russia who lived with them.

When Grandmom stood before us in her shoes and dress, her skin looked laundered smooth. With her face framed in lace, you'd almost think she was still a bride. She'd stand and point to the old framed wedding photograph that used to hang on the wall. It showed a young man with licorice-black, slick hair, his arm draped around his bride. "He was such a sweet man," she'd say. "Always gave you kids candy. Remember?"

P. J. remembered because she's two years older. I was only four when he died in 1951, so I had only shriveled memories.

Now there was a different wedding picture on the wall. I ran my finger over the jagged edge of the paper and traced the outline of the smiling man waving his purple-banner bride.

Marc Chagall? I looked at my sister. Why was she nodding like she knew who he was?

"He looks happy," said P. J., "but there's a funny expression on your face, Grandmom, like you were dizzy or maybe afraid he was going to let go of your hand. Were you scared?"

"No, P. J. He'd never let me go."

Why were they pretending these were real people? "Grandmom," I said, "that's not you. Where are your white shoes?" When she didn't answer, my lower lip did a shimmy shake. "Why are you making stuff up?"

"Cookie, what are you talking about? Don't you recognize Vitebsk?"

Grandmom barely had an accent, so it was easy to forget she'd come from somewhere else. She may have talked to P. J. about the famous artist who came from the same town, but

I'd heard her mention the name Marc only once before, and I didn't recognize Vitebsk as I stood in Grandmom's bedroom hovering at the intersection of real and make believe.

"That's just a stupid painting," I said. "Where's the *real* picture? The *real* you?"

P. J. stood next to Grandmom's rocking chair, looking at me with *shut up* all over her face.

"Tell her that people don't fly, P. J.," I said. My sister was so smart, she never even believed in Santa Claus. That's why she was going to be a lawyer, like Daddy was. "Tell her, P. J.," I yelled.

Grandmom rocked slowly, mumbling as if she were praying.

"Cookie, it's time for the cake," P. J. called instead, bringing Grandmom and me back to the moment. "You can do the honors." It was my turn to perform the closing ritual in Grandmom's pared-down wedding reenactment.

I unwrapped a pack of Tastykakes, handing one chocolate cupcake to P. J. and taking one for myself before giving the wrapper with the remaining cupcake to Grandmom. She peeled off the cupcake and ate it as P. J. and I ate ours and then licked the chocolate icing off the paper. "Wrapper icing is the best thing about Tastykakes," she said, wiping her mouth with a Happy Anniversary napkin. The party was over.

The Ventnor library smelled like old paper marinated in sea salt. I wandered around the children's room waiting for the librarian to turn her back so I could sneak into the adult section. The librarian was a shriveled stump of a woman with a seagull beak and a voice made for shushing and shooing. You had to be thirteen to read the grown-up stuff, but I didn't care. If I wanted to be a reporter like Brenda Starr in the comics, I'd have to start bending stupid rules. What kind of dirty stuff did they think I'd find in art books, except maybe pictures of naked ladies? I already knew how they looked. Like a good reporter, I'd brought a notebook to record the facts about Marc Chagall, the mysterious painter from Russia who drew flying people and who may or may not have been married to my grandmother.

The oversized art books were lying flat on a bottom shelf. I pulled out the one on Chagall and crouched in a corner. The book was printed on glossy paper, even the text part. There was a short section about his life, but it was mostly pictures— people flying, men playing fiddles, weird-looking animals. I stared at a painting of a guy in a white suit with a sad, upside-down head. Behind the man were some houses like the ones in Grandmom's poster, except these were black. The words "Ox Bowe" were printed at the bottom in funny letters. There was a jagged gap in the binding where a page had been ripped out.

The photograph of Chagall in the book showed a curly-haired man who didn't look anything like slick-haired Grand-pop in Grandmom's old wedding photo. Chagall had moved to Paris and married a woman named Bella, who'd died many years ago. Grandmom was still alive and her name wasn't Bella, so she couldn't have been married to Chagall.

"You knew she made it up," I told P. J. later that afternoon.

"She believes she was married to him."

"That's impossible."

"Anything's possible if you believe it, Cookie."

"You're not making any sense, P. J. I thought you wanted to be a lawyer."

"I do."

"Well, you don't sound like one to me."

If Mom had gotten her way, her mother wouldn't have moved in with us. I know because I heard her arguing with Daddy late one night.

"She can't stay where she is, Sonia. They'll rob her blind," he said.

"We could set her up in an apartment."

"But you promised you'd never leave her alone. Signed on the dotted line."

"She wouldn't be alone in an apartment."

"Alone is alone." Dad was probably thinking of his own mother, who'd been found dead in her apartment a day after suffering a stroke.

"I know I signed, but is it legally binding?"

"Technically you'll have to give up your chunk of the estate if you don't abide by the agreement."

Mom sounded beaten. "It won't be pretty, the two of us in the same house."

Before Grandmom moved in with us, she lived in Philadelphia's Overbrook Park section, close to the suburbs. Grandmom and Grandpop had converted the basement of their row house into a dress shop. We'd visited as often as Mom would take us. The room was crammed with racks of dresses, blouses, skirts, and gowns. When there were no customers, Grandmom let P. J., Susan, and me pick dresses off the racks and try them on in the laundry-cum-fitting room. P. J. was chunky like Grandmom, with light skin and freckles. Her hair, once defiantly red, had betrayed her by the time she was ten, turning a weak coffee brown. I was dark and thin like Mom. Susan, with her straight blond hair and porcelain skin, resembled no one in the family. Soon she'd be decked out in a strapless gown with a beaded top she had yet to grow into, tottering around in the high-heeled shoes Grandmom had scattered around for the ladies. Susan was molding herself into the nickname she'd been given.

When P. J. and I got tired of dressing up, we'd duck under racks, pretending we were lost in the jungle. We'd undress the mannequins, laughing at their flattened lady parts. Mom always waited for us upstairs. I wondered if she'd ever played downstairs when she was growing up in that same house or whether then, like now, the clothing business had been beneath her.

We behaved ourselves when customers came into the shop. P. J. and I watched Grandmom size up the ladies with her eyes, the way artists on the boardwalk draw someone's picture in five brushstrokes; then she'd hand them the skirt or dress they were meant to have. Her regulars didn't even bother scanning the racks.

"How do you do it, Grandmom?"

"One part art, P. J., to three parts practice."

"What about magic?"

Grandmom shook her head side to side, but her smile suggested that magic might indeed be a part of the equation.

When Grandmom first moved into our house on the Main Line, she wandered ghostlike from room to room.

"It's not like you don't know this place," Mom complained. "You've been here hundreds of times."

"So many rooms. It's like a castle."

"Three thousand square feet. Not much compared to some of the other houses in the neighborhood."

"Well, I prefer the summer house in Ventnor. This place feels like a dress that's three sizes too big."

"Momma, would you stop with the dresses already. You're out of the clothing business." Mom made the word "clothing" sound like something slimy you'd find under a trash can.

When Grandmom wandered our house, I'd always think she was looking for the house she'd left behind and the shop where she'd worked her magic. We asked her what she'd done with the clothing, but she wouldn't say. I pictured her plucking the racks as if they were chickens, feeding her regulars one last time, until there was nothing left but metal bones.

The night after Grandmom moved in, P. J. and I sat at the foot of her bed as she rubbed Nivea into her arms and neck.

"I remember things," she said, eyes half closed. "Russia. The smell of the cows and the way it looked when the sun went down, like the church steeples were on fire. Papa blessing the bread. He was so smart, studying all day." Her voice trailed off.

When I asked Mom the next day if she'd known Grandmom had come from a different country, she shrugged. "That was a long time ago. I heard those stories plenty when I was younger."

A few nights later, I heard voices in Grandmom's room. Through the half-open door, I saw P. J. and Grandmom in bed, laughing.

"You started telling your stories without me!" I cried, sounding like the little kid I used to be, the one who'd tagged along behind her big sisters, squawking, "Me, too."

Sometimes I noticed Susan staring at P. J. and me when we talked and horsed around together. I wasn't sure what I saw in her eyes, but I thought I understood how she felt—the same way I felt watching Grandmom and P. J. laughing in the bedroom.

Grandmom's stories began with her childhood in Vitebsk and ended when she got married, as if those were the starting and ending points of her life. She told us about the crossing, and how her father had died on the ship, but she didn't speak of Marc Chagall.

Some nights, after we'd gone to bed, I'd hear footsteps in the hall and then voices on the other side of the wall. I don't think Grandmom intentionally left me out. It's just that I floated just outside her range of vision, like something in a Chagall painting. She seemed to find a kindred spirit in P. J. I saw how she smoothed P. J.'s hair and told her how smart she was, something she did for me with less intensity. I resented Grandmom's intrusion into our lives and the way she made me feel like an outsider with my favorite sister. I discovered that if I brushed my hair over the right half of my face and looked to the left, I could make Grandmom disappear.

Two weeks after the anniversary party in Ventnor, Grandmom went missing for the first time. P. J. and I knew something was wrong as soon as we walked up the porch steps with a Necco Sky Bar and two Archie comics and saw the empty rocking chair. Grandmom had given us money to go buy chocolate, and until that moment, we'd thought she'd never pass up a chocolate opportunity. So, if Grandmom wasn't sitting in her chair on the screened-in porch, she was either in the bathroom or napping in her room. But she wasn't in either of those places.

The call came from the Ventnor police department just as Mom walked in with a bag of groceries. They said the librarian had reported an old lady wandering around the stacks wearing a bathing suit backwards. The policeman who answered the call recognized Grandmom. He'd covered her with a striped beach towel, but by the time he got her home, the towel had slipped off one shoulder, and a wrinkled Grandmom booby bounced up and down like a Slinky. Mom scolded her, P. J. hugged her, and I wondered if I'd ever grow boobies. And if I did, would they look like that?

Mom was afraid Grandmom had Alzheimer's and told us girls we all needed to keep an eye on her. I looked up the ten signs of Alzheimer's in the library. Except for the wandering, she didn't have any of the symptoms described in the book, though there were other changes in her behavior, like how she cut her wedding veil into strips and knit them into an afghan. I wondered if she was just living in her own world because she didn't want to live in this one anymore.

But she still loved the beach, sitting in her chair under the umbrella, and looking up to watch the Goodyear blimp or planes towing advertising banners. We sat with her by the water's edge in beach chairs so low the water splashed our butts through the webbing when the tide came in.

"Look at that," she said one afternoon, pointing to a boy flying a dragon-shaped kite that spit a paper tongue of fire as it swooped. "Marc did a kite painting, but that man is sitting on a roof when he flies his kite." She drew some letters in the sand: Ox Bowe.

"What's that?" I asked.

"Och Bosheh. It's Russian."

"What's it mean?"

"Oh, God," she sighed.

The second time Grandmom wandered off, we found her on the roof of the lifeguard house where they stored rescue equipment. It was late, and the beach was deserted. Grandmom was leaning back against the sloped roof, her feet resting on the gutter, which was all that kept her from sliding off. We begged her to stand still and stay calm as Dad ran back to the house to call the police. She stared past us.

"Jesus H. Christ," the cop said as he walked down the ramp to the beach. "How'd she do that? There's no ladder or nothing. She musta swung herself over the boardwalk railing onto the roof."

"Or she flew," P. J. suggested. That was the last time I saw Grandmom smile.

She was too high up for anyone to reach, and the lifeguard house was locked, so Dad ran back to the house to get a ladder. As he set the ladder against the side of the building, Grandmom sidestepped along the gutter to the front of the building, spread her arms, and flew. The sand was soft and deep, so she hardly made a sound as she landed on her side.

"Hip fractures can be deadly," the doctor told my mother a couple of days later. "She might never make it out of the hospital. We'll try to keep her as comfortable as possible and move her to a private room when one becomes available."

Mom and Dad filled her room with flowers, and P.J. and I brought chocolate bars when we visited. P. J. spent as much time as she could at her bedside. That was P. J.'s gift to Grandmom. I realized there was something I could give her too. Something I'd owed her ever since I'd tried to make her disappear, if only in my imagination.

The staff had already transferred Grandmom's belongings to the single room she'd be moving to the following day. Grandmom had lots of visitors that night, so no one noticed when I slipped out of the crowded room carrying a canvas tote.

Walking into Grandmom's new room, I unrolled the pictures I'd ripped out of the Chagall book from the library and taped them to the walls—flying cows, and couples, and fiddlers, and horses—until the room danced. Then I climbed onto the nightstand and taped the ragged-edged wedding picture to the ceiling over her bed, so she could look at herself floating high above the village, with Marc Chagall holding her firmly by the hand.

By The Numbers

Find the slope of the line y=1/2x+1.

The familiar panic lodged in Allison's gut as she chose an answer on the screen. That one was easy—she was sure she got it right—but Allison knew what was coming. Her math psychologist had taught her to think positively, but why bother? All the tutoring and positive thinking in the world couldn't make her a math whiz.

Two six-sided dice are rolled. What's the probability that the first dice comes up 2 and the second comes up 5?

What was the probability she'd pass this time? Her brother had passed on the first try. Thanks to a lucky roll of the genetic dice, Josh had inherited their father's math gene; once he finished his robotics degree, there'd be a good job waiting for him. What would be waiting for her?

I can do this. I can DO this. She struggled for air. Relax. Breathe in for four, hold for seven, out for eight. Through the mouth. Whoosh. Four-seven-eight, four-seven-eight. Too many numbers.

Prove that from a point A outside a circle it is possible to draw exactly two tangents to the circle and...

Now comes the *real* math, she thought, as anxiety

pinwheeled in her chest. This was her third and final attempt to pass the test.

"Don't panic," her mother had told her the previous night. "Positive thinking—that's the key. It worked for me when I took—"

"The SATs, Mom? We both know that's ancient history." Ancient History. One of the many subjects that had disappeared since The Policy was instituted and the government had started shutting down liberal-arts programs.

Function f is such that f(-x)=f(x) and differentiable...

Her heart pounded. Four-seven-eight. Whoosh. Time to start guessing. Josh wouldn't have to guess. *It's not fair.*

"It's not the end of the world if you don't pass," her mother said hopefully.

"Yes it is. Who's going to hire me, if I don't pass?"

Allison's mother put her arms around her daughter and whispered, "I'm sure someone will."

If F(x) is an antiderivative of f(x), then...

The writing was on the wall—literally. The exam room was plastered with the same slogans and statistics she'd been fed since grade school. "STEM grads get jobs." "Do something good for your country: Study Science, Technology, Engineering, or Math." "Nerds, your the wave of the future." Did anyone even notice the spelling error? Or care?

When Allison was a sophomore in high school, two of her stories had been published in national literary journals. The guidance counselor told her she had a gift and urged her to apply to all the writing programs in the country, which wasn't hard, since there were so few of them left.

By the time the rejections arrived (*Though your work is impressive...so few spaces available...only the truly exceptional...wish you luck elsewhere*), Congress had voted to stop subsidizing non-STEM education. "Those people are a drain on the economy," said the Speaker of the House. "We need to stop flushing money down the toilet and give it to the best and the brightest—the ones who will make our country great again." The following year,

Congress voted The Policy into law.

What would she do with her life? Wait tables? Babysit old people? The words on the screen blurred, and she swiped away tears with the back of her hand. She reread the question and guessed the answer, not even bothering with the calculator. What was the point?

A mechanical voice announced "Time," and the screens went dark. Allison put her head down on the desk and listened to what the others said as they filed out.

"Not as bad as I thought."

"Much easier the second time."

"What was the answer to—"

The upbeat voices faded, leaving her alone with the computers and slogans.

Most of the chairs in the waiting room were filled with grim-faced young people like Allison, accompanied by their grim-faced parents. No one spoke, read magazines, or tapped away at their phones. The silence was broken only when the receptionist called a name.

When Allison was called, her mother embraced her. "You can still have a good life," she said, tears streaking her cheeks.

"No, I can't. Not now. Not ever."

She was crying when the nurse led her into the pre-op area and handed her a gown. "Opens in front, dear."

All that work, thought Allison, clutching the gown, white knuckled. Perfect grades except for math, and they treat me like I'm mentally defective.

"No." Allison threw the gown back at the nurse. "You can't do this to me."

She ran toward the door, but the nurse grabbed her shoulder. "I'm so sorry," she said. Her voice was gentle, her grip firm. "I don't like it either, but you know The Policy."

"It's not fair."

"I know, I know," said the nurse soothingly as she helped Allison remove her clothes and put on the gown.

The smell of disinfectant and latex assailed her as she lay on the gurney and thought about the wonderful life her brother would enjoy. A good job. A family. *If The Policy had been in place when Mom was my age,* she thought, *I'd never have been born.* Left alone, Allison cried out all her anger and frustration; by the time the doctor came in, all that was left was an icy patina of resignation.

The doctor had a kind face. Was this what he'd had in mind when he went to med school—sterilizing healthy young people who had the misfortune to be born with talents that were now obsolete?

"I'm going to inject anesthesia," he said, "and I want you to count backward from a hundred."

The corners of her mouth turned up in what might have been a smile. *Finally, a math problem I can handle,* she thought before closing her eyes. "Ninety-nine, ninety-eight, ninety-sev..."

Flightless Bird

Karla was in the attic, sorting and discarding, when a bluesy guitar riff from downstairs hitched itself to a draft of hot air and rode it up to her. Karla would have preferred to unburden in silence, or, if pressed, to a classical soundtrack. She might have been more receptive to the music had it not been coming from the childhood bedroom of her thirty-one-year-old daughter, Phoebe, who'd once told her and Jack she'd only be staying a couple of months, until she got back on her feet. That's what she'd said the last time, when she ended up staying eight months.

Karla had already gotten rid of the easy stuff—broken toys, baby clothes, cocktail dresses with shoulder pads, encyclopedias, party decorations. But the room was still littered with cartons and trash bags and more stuff to sort. At the moment, she was working on a pile of yellowed newspapers with banner headlines that catalogued the major events of the sixties, seventies, and eighties. History reduced to a fire hazard. She'd planned to toss the whole heap into the recycle bin but couldn't resist looking at some of the headlines one more time.

December 8, 1980. *John Lennon Shot Dead*. Hard to believe he'd been gone fifteen years.

June 18, 1983. *Sally Ride, First American Woman in Space*. She sneezed as she brushed dust off the picture of the astronaut in her blue spacesuit, smiling out into history from the space shuttle. Karla opened the dormer window, shielded her eyes, and looked out the pie-slice opening. The neighborhood was dark enough for her to make out Cassiopeia's familiar zig-zag cluster of stars above the trees. Tonight, the constellation showed herself as a W, but sometimes she hung upside-down—punishment for her vanity, according to the myth. Karla had learned about the constellations as a child from what had been her favorite book, *Our Starland*.

It's here somewhere, she thought. She moved over to the books crammed into the huge bookcase lining the far wall. Shouldn't be hard to spot, with its royal blue cover and white star map of Ursa Major. Its pages would be yellowed with age, worn ragged from her countless reading and rereading of those stories. That bright blue cover shouldn't be hard to—a husky female voice from below interrupted her thoughts, wailing an unfamiliar tune.

Phoebe and her partner, or boyfriend, or whatever he was, had recently suffered a string of bad luck. They'd been counting on income from a recording that had encountered "technical difficulties" in the final stages of production. Then they'd taken a financial hit from the cancellation of a big concert in St. Louis and another in New Orleans. Karla had no idea what "big" meant. For all she knew, a coffeehouse was a big venue to Phoebe. What did the girl expect, choosing a career as a singer-songwriter? Karla shoved the rest of the newspapers back into the carton and interlaced the top flaps.

Karla and Jack had argued when Phoebe asked if she could move back in.

"Give her a break, Karlie," Jack had said. "She's following her dreams."

"Don't you think it's time for her to wake up and get a real job?"

"This *is* her job."

"So she says."

"Have you ever actually listened to her music? Met her fans? Are you even aware that they play her in the regular rotation on WXPN?"

"But she still can't afford her own place. Oh, hell. At least this time she didn't ask if her boyfriend could stay here, too."

They played and replayed this argument in regular rotation. Sometimes the recurring tropes of their marriage were like those annoying lyrics that stayed etched in memory. Almost, but not quite, enough to drive you crazy.

When Phoebe was under their roof, Karla often felt the weight of the attic bearing down on her. Sometimes, as she lay in bed with Jack snoring softly next to her, she wrestled with images of the attic floor giving way and crushing her in her sleep. Once she got rid of enough stuff, she and Jack would be able to sell this house and move on to the next phase of their lives. When she asked Jack to help her, he said he'd be happy to, once they actually started looking for a new place. But she didn't want to wait. Each time Phoebe came home, Karla took to the attic to get rid of things.

Karla went downstairs and listened outside her daughter's room. It sounded like Phoebe was working on a new song— humming a line, fitting a set of words to the melody, tweaking it, and then moving on to the next line. Phoebe had a voice made for the blues, a little Janis Joplin, a little Bonnie Raitt. But how many Janis and Bonnie wannabees were out there, competing for the same sliver of glory? Still, there was something haunting about this particular melody, the way it switched unexpectedly from minor to major.

I should tell her I like it. Try to be a good mother. A supportive mother. Karla knocked. The music stopped.

"Mom? What—"

"Can I come in?"

"Um...sure." Phoebe didn't sound at all sure.

Karla stretched her neck to relieve the tension and then

opened the door. Phoebe was sitting on the double bed, arms crossed over the side of the guitar that rested on her lap, her long, straight hair hanging like a ginger curtain over her shoulders. She had her father's Irish coloring and delicate features— none of the darker shades of hair and skin from Karla's Mediterranean side of the family. Where Phoebe's hair was straight, Karla's was curly. Phoebe's body was lean and tall, while Karla was all curves. Except for a straight nose and full lips, they shared no physical attributes.

How many years since she and Phoebe had sat on that bed, hunched over the book with the stars on the cover? How many galaxies lay between the two of them now?

"What's up?" Phoebe's green eyes narrowed, belying her casual tone.

"Just wanted to tell you that sounded nice. What you were just playing was so—"

"It's new," she replied in a monotone before looking down at the guitar and lightly plucking the E string with her thumbnail.

Silence. Karla didn't know where to go from there. She could have asked Phoebe to play a little more for her, complimented her artistry, said what parents were supposed to say to encourage their children. But Phoebe was no longer a child, and Karla was out of the practice of complimenting her daughter.

Phoebe raised her head but didn't make eye contact. "Hunter and I are going to try this song out in a couple weeks. You should come see us play. We'll be at TLA on South Street."

This wasn't the first time Phoebe had invited her to one of their concerts. But Karla didn't think she could endure standing in a crowd of tattooed, tank-topped kids half her age. Even the ones who were younger than her daughter probably had master's degrees, kids, careers.

"Dad and I talked about it. Maybe we'll both come," Karla said, trying for a note of cheeriness. But she'd hesitated too long.

"Yeah, right. Like all the other times. You haven't seen me perform since I was in college."

"That's not true."

"Is true. Unless you snuck in and I missed you," said Phoebe with a smirking half-smile.

Karla blushed.

"Why can't you be happy for me, Mom? Support me?" Her voice was soft as a prayer.

"I *do* support you. You're staying here, aren't you, not even paying rent, until you...get your act together."

"Why don't you just put air quotes around that?" She attacked the guitar strings with her pick and sang out loud and tunelessly, "She wants me to go."

"Phoebe, that's not—"

"She wants me to go," Phoebe repeated, upping the volume with each iteration as her pick mercilessly rode the open strings.

"You can stay as long as you need to." Karla, red-faced, struggled to be heard above her daughter's outburst. Shame turned to anger as Phoebe continued her musical rage.

"Damn it, Phoebe, why are you wasting your life?" She'd lost control of her mouth. "You were a physics major. Graduated Summa, for God's sake. You could be doing something with—"

Phoebe yelled something incomprehensible, the smack of her hand against the guitar delivering a death blow to the conversation.

As the edges of the room grew hazy through her tears, Karla turned and walked out. She should have known how the conversation would end—the way all their conversations had ended since her daughter had chosen music over science and common sense. Over the years, it had gotten harder for Karla to parse her complicated relationship with Phoebe, to sift through the anger to get to the love part. Sometimes she had to remind herself that she loved her daughter.

Jack was away on a business trip, or he'd have laced into Karla and then negotiated an armed truce between mother and daughter, just as her own father had been a buffer between her and her mother. Now it was up to Karla to raise the white flag and apologize to her daughter, to tell her that she and Jack would attend her upcoming gig. She'd do it tomorrow. She needed air.

She walked downstairs to the side porch and settled into an old wicker rocking chair, wrapping herself in a thin blanket against the early spring chill. Though only a sliver of sky was visible through the treetops, she set about constructing a map of the stars in her head, a technique she'd used to calm herself since she was a teenager. By that time, she'd graduated from *Our Starland* to college astronomy textbooks. Back then, whenever someone asked her what she wanted to do with her life, she gave the answer she'd been giving for as long as she could remember: "I want to fly rockets."

But we don't always get what we wish for, she thought. She looked up at the sky, but clouds had rolled in and she could no longer see the stars. She got up and went inside.

Skylab Analytics had been unusually quiet all morning, until a phone rang in a nearby cube and its occupant struck up a conversation in a clueless outside voice. Karla pushed her chair back from the computer table, stood up, and flashed a "not again" eye roll over the cube divider to her friend Trish, who worked in the cube behind her. Trish responded in kind. The cubicles were laid out like rows of tract housing. Someone in the vast, open workspace shushed the loud talker, who reduced her volume to a stage whisper.

Back when Karla was an undergraduate at Drexel University and was interning at Skylab, she'd had her own private office. Everyone had. But soon after she left, they tore down the walls to encourage cooperation, or as one bullshit expert put it, "to get people to share by forcing them to bump into each other, setting off sparks of creativity." For the most part, all the workers shared was stale air, loud music, and the overhearing of uncomfortably personal phone conversations.

Karla had returned to Skylab after a three-year stint as a high school teacher. Her twenty years there had earned her a cube by a window. She wrote software for rocket engines that thrust people into space, while herself being imprisoned by windows that didn't open. She loved the design work, the modeling, even the programming. But this wasn't how she'd pictured herself flying rockets when she was younger. She no longer minded; she'd come to believe that an essential part of growing up meant whittling childish expectations down to adult size.

It was lunchtime anyway, so Karla and Trish headed for the cafeteria. They'd been friends since their undergraduate days at Drexel and lunched together most afternoons. Trish bore a strong resemblance to the young Shirley Temple, down to the dimple on her cheek. People were always surprised to learn that someone so *perky,* as they'd put it, had earned a Ph.D. in astrophysics at Penn. The two of them avoided talking shop whenever possible, since the work could be draining, so anyone overhearing their usual lunchtime conversation would have no idea they crafted complex algorithms for a living.

They found a table in the crowded lunchroom, placing their trays at their seats. "You watching that new doctor series on Thursday night?" Karla picked up her tuna wrap.

"*Chicago General*? Yeah. I can relate to it." Trish ripped the edge off a packet of Italian dressing and poured it on her salad. Then she speared a carrot and popped it into her mouth.

"What do you mean?" Karla realized her mistake the moment she asked the question. Now the conversation would shift to Trish's amazing son. She put the wrap back down on her plate.

Trish held up a hand until she chewed the carrot and swallowed it. "Remember the episode where dreamy doctor what's-his-name saves the life of that ambassador who's trying to broker a huge peace deal?"

Karla nodded, bracing herself.

"Funny thing. Just last week, Todd performed orthoscopic

surgery on a Saudi Arabian prince who refused to let anyone else operate on his back."

As Trish filled in the details of her son's encounter with the prince and recounted how he had offered Todd and his family a week's vacation on his yacht in gratitude for his excellent outcome, Karla couldn't stop a tentacle of envy from wrapping itself around her chest. She took a deep breath.

Karla knew her friend was just continuing the conversation they'd begun years earlier about their children. Back then, Karla had hoped that Phoebe would get over her garage-band phase and move on to something real, like Trish's two boys and her other friends' children had. All of them had grown up, gotten married, and produced grandchildren. But Phoebe had taken the road less traveled, and that had made all the damn difference.

"So what's new with Phoebe?" Trish asked at last. "She's such a fabulous musician."

Was that a note of condescension in her friend's voice? No, Karla was imagining it. Her friend would never address her with condescension. She told Trish about the upcoming concert at the TLA as they finished their lunch. But she didn't ask that her friend meet her at the concert, since she wasn't sure she'd be going herself.

That night, Karla ascended to the attic again and began sorting through one last carton of her own items; next she would dive into the sea of unfulfilled promise that was her daughter's memorabilia. The carton was crammed full of her old math and science textbooks, advanced ones Karla had saved to share with Phoebe when her daughter was old enough to appreciate them. But the window of appreciation had slammed shut long ago. Since the library didn't accept used textbooks as donations, she'd have to chuck them. At the bottom of the carton she found her old GRE study guide. Karla had started prepping for the exam when she was a college junior and living at home. She'd been determined to work her way through her master's and Ph.D., and then apply to NASA's astronaut training program. They'd just begun to accept women with no flying experience. Karla riffled through the guide, its pages annotated with pencil marks and margin notes. At first, she'd spent several nights a week studying for the GRE in her bedroom. Then her father died. She'd continued her studies in the den that had once been his study, a small room filled with towering bookcases and a massive oak desk. To some, the atmosphere would have been suffocating. But Karla felt the lingering memory of her father embrace her whenever she sat in his soft leather chair.

One spring night, her mother, uncharacteristically tight-lipped and uncomfortable, appeared at the door. "We've got to talk."

"Can it wait five minutes?" Karla asked. "I'm just finishing this practice test."

Her mother said nothing but didn't turn away.

"Okay," said Karla with a sigh of annoyance, putting her pencil down a little harder than she intended. She gave her attention to her mother.

"I know you've been counting on our...my help to pay for your tuition." Beads of sweat dotted her mother's neck, despite the air conditioning.

Karla nodded. Her parents had promised her they'd foot the bill for her graduate school tuition and room and board, as long as she got the grades.

"I don't know how else to say this, so I'm going to come out with it. That money's gone." Her mother said the words so softly that at first, Karla wasn't sure she'd heard correctly. "What do you mean?" Karla asked, feeling her stomach tighten.

"I just can't afford it now. You're on your own." Her mother's expression was icy.

That made no sense. A year earlier, shortly before his death, her father had shown her a statement from the education savings account they'd been using to pay her college tuition. "Wherever you want to go to graduate school," he'd told her, "there's money to cover it." She'd seen the balance in that account. Not only that, but after her father's death, she'd overheard her mother telling a friend that he'd left her with a generous pension and a life insurance settlement. But it didn't surprise Karla that her mother wasn't going to support her dream.

"Really? No money in my education account?" She didn't try to hide the sarcasm in her voice. "I've got an idea. Why don't you show me the bank book?" Karla held out her hand as if her mother were carrying it in her back pocket.

Red patches spread across her mother's cheeks.

Karla looked at the poster of Alan Shepard that she'd tacked up on the den wall. Her mother followed her gaze and narrowed her eyes. "Flying's a man's game," she said.

"Like I haven't been playing a man's game?" Karla closed the practice book. "You think it's a picnic being the only girl in my advanced science classes? Sexist comments, even when you get the highest grades?"

"You and your women's lib. You think feminism started with your generation."

"No. I—"

"Let me tell you." She pointed at Karla. "*I'm* the feminist. Don't look at me like that. You didn't live through the Depression. You didn't see what happened to the gals whose husbands lost everything."

"This isn't the Depression. And we aren't 'gals.'" She air-quoted. "We're 'women' opening up 'men's' professions."

"Gal, woman, whatever. You're looking at how many years—four—before you can even apply to be an astronaut? And then there's a good chance you won't get in, what with all the competition, and … even if you do, you'll probably find it harder to get a man. Most men would be too intimidated to marry a female astronaut."

Karla gripped the sides of her father's battered desk,

frustration building at her mother's tunnel vision. "You really think that? For God's sake, times have changed."

"Uh-uh," said her mother, shaking her head side to side. "When it comes to women's lives, things don't change. We're wives and mothers first. You think the men are going to stay home and take care of the kids? That's why you need to do something more secure. Like…like teaching. Something you can go back to after you have children."

"Who said I want to teach? Or even want children?"

"*Want* has nothing to do with it." She put her hands on her hips. "You do what you have to do. Think I wanted to be a parochial school teacher? That's all I could get without a degree." She took a deep breath before continuing in a softer voice. "But you…you'll have a degree, and some of those suburban districts pay big bucks. Great pensions. So…"

Her mother hesitated so long Karla thought she had no more to say. But then: "If you want to go on and get your master's in teaching, there might be some money for that. You could do that in one year."

Karla was on her feet. "Suddenly there's money for a teaching degree. Money for what *you* want me to be. But what *I* want isn't worth shit."

"Karla. That's uncalled for," her mother shouted, a vein pulsing in her throat.

Karla picked up the study guide. "I guess I won't be needing this anymore," she said, slamming the book down on the desk. Her mother left the doorway, probably on her way to the kitchen. "I don't need *you* either," Karla yelled after her. "I can take care of myself."

"I can take care of myself," she repeated softly, slumping back into her father's

chair. By now, the memory of him had deserted her, and the walls of the overstuffed room were closing in. She shut her eyes and took deep cleansing breaths.

Inhale. Step one: Get accepted into grad school. *Exhale.*

Inhale. Step two: Apply for scholarships and loans. *Exhale.*

Inhale. Step three: Get a second job. *Exhale.*

Inhale. Step four: Move out of this damn house. *Exhale.*

Karla had never suffered from test anxiety before. But the two times she took the GRE, confidence drained out of her, as if she'd been pricked full of holes. She sat in the examination room thinking, *What if I'm not as smart as I thought? And if I let my mother make me feel helpless, it's obvious I don't have what it takes to make it as an astronaut.* Steeped in negative thoughts, she couldn't remember answers to things she used to know without hesitation. So, she didn't have a good enough score to apply to graduate school. She never got past step one.

Karla realized she was still clutching the study guide—the last item in the last box of personal items—though she'd had every intention of chucking it and heading downstairs. She leafed through pages of math and science questions whose answers were so obvious now. After graduating from Drexel with a degree in physics, she took a teaching job, figuring she'd stay long enough to get her mojo back, and then the school system would reimburse her for graduate courses. But after long days in a cash-strapped, inner-city school, where she often had to fill in for absent teachers along with teaching her own classes, she'd been too drained to study. And after a three-year absence from test taking, when she finally took the GRE again, her scores were even worse. Luckily, scores didn't matter on the job market. She applied for a job at Skylab, where she'd interned as an undergraduate, and they welcomed her back. They even paid for the advanced coursework she needed to move up the ladder.

No more dreams of training as an astronaut. Her inability to jump the hurdle her mother had planted in her path was proof that she lacked the "right stuff." And once she'd gotten married and had a child of her own, she no longer doubted her path. Karla enjoyed motherhood more than she could ever have imagined. Phoebe was a delightful child, curious and creative. The life of an astronaut would most likely have consumed evenings and weekends, and she'd have missed out on so much.

The remaining cartons held Phoebe's memorabilia. Quickly she looked through a box loaded with honor-roll certificates, academic awards, and blue ribbons from science fairs. The next box held buttons, T-shirts, and posters from the various bands Phoebe had been in—*Cassiopeia, Space Angels, The Phoebe Collective*—each group rising phoenix-like from the ashes of the previous one. Karla unrolled a creased poster advertising a gig at a long-defunct bar called Duke's, back when Phoebe was a senior at Penn. Karla remembered that place. A dive so saturated with cigarette smoke it would have choked the Marlboro Man. Who said Karla had never supported her daughter? She'd hung out at lots of places like that to see Phoebe perform—sometimes with Jack, sometimes alone. Her ears rang for days after from the over-amped music. And she'd never expressed disapproval of her daughter's career choice by withholding money, as her own mother had done. Just the thought of that hostile act stoked the embers of an anger she thought she'd extinguished.

Jack's hacking cough interrupted her thoughts. Karla had promised to go to Phoebe's performance at the TLA with him, but he'd come back from his business trip with a nasty virus. Though the cough, red nose, and fever were genuine, he got sick so rarely she was tempted to accuse him of malingering just to get her to go to the concert alone. Instead, she pushed aside the carton she was looking through and went downstairs to get some fluids into him.

She tiptoed into the spare room where he was staying till he recovered. Jack's eyes were closed. The shades were drawn, and the carpet muffled her footsteps. But when she set a glass of water down on the nightstand, he opened his eyes.

"You look like something's on your mind," he said.

Despite his watery eyes, he could read her so well. She hated to bring up something difficult while he was so sick, but he'd given her the opening.

She pulled a chair up next to the bed and sat down. "I...I just can't go without you."

"Karla, we promised." He sat up with difficulty, his face flushed with fever, his gray-flecked red hair flattened against his scalp.

She did her best to keep the frustration out of her voice. "*We* promised. Now it's just me."

"What's the problem with that?" He sneezed and pulled a tissue out of the box beside him. "What are you afraid of?" He blew his nose and threw the tissue into a wastebasket three-quarters full.

"Not afraid. Just...awkward. Me and a mob of twenty-somethings wondering, *What the hell is she doing here*?" He closed his eyes and shook his head slowly in exasperation.

"What?"

"What's this really about, Karla?"

"You know what it's about. It's about why can't she just grow up, like the rest of her friends?"

"Sounds like something your mother would have told you."

"That's a cheap shot. It's not the same at all. When my mother said she wasn't going to finance my 'childish dreams,' she pulled the purse strings tight. That sound like the way I... we treat Phoebe?"

Jack shook his head.

"No," continued Karla. "We gave her money to do her thing. Money we'd saved for her college education. It floated her for a year when she moved to Nashville. And we don't make her pay rent when she lives at home, like I had to do. So don't you dare tell me I sound like my mother."

"Okay," he said, waving a clean tissue as a truce flag. "But when she wanted to go to Berklee College of Music, I was willing to take on a little debt to help pay her tuition, but you resisted—at least at first. You claimed paying for a music college would be 'enabling her.' I think you actually said something about the music biz being a costly addiction."

"Isn't it?" She picked up the water glass and handed it to him. "Anyway, I agreed to go along with your offer."

He took a sip and held the glass out. "And then she decided not to go, so..."

She crossed her arms. "Drink it all."

"Yes, Mother," he said. He drank the water down.

"You know," she said as he put down the glass, "my mother was right."

"I can't believe—"

"She was. She told me to get a good, safe job, and I did. We'd have gone under when you lost your job if I hadn't been working a real job."

"Not true. We would've—"

"Who would have paid the bills? The insurance premiums? Who was the breadwinner? If Phoebe has kids, how will she take care of them without a real job?" She was yelling now.

A door slammed across the hall, the sound hitting Karla like a slap in the face, stopping the words she'd been unable to hold back. Words that were a heritage from her mother. Words that she was now passing on to her daughter, who had heard every one of them. "I'm sorry, Jack." She leaned down and kissed his forehead.

I'm sorry, Phoebe.

He stayed silent.

"Okay," she whispered. "I'll go to the TLA by myself."

Karla parked her car a couple of blocks from the theater and slowly made her way down South Street, dodging clumps of young people. The TLA marquee was visible from a distance, but she had to make her way past clubs, bars, galleries, and two condom shops before she got close enough to make out the words **Tonight only: The Dinosaurs.** Beneath it in smaller type: **Phoebe-Hunter.** A hyphen bolted the two names together. When had that happened?

She bought a ticket and walked into a lobby packed with young people bursting with Friday-night exuberance. Though it was April, the night was chilly; Mother Nature hadn't gotten the message that spring had arrived. Still, many of the girls wore tank tops. Lucky for them the lobby was overheated, though their young blood was probably immune to the cold anyway.

Karla unzipped her jacket and took a deep breath, inhaling a heady mix of smoke, sweat, and cosmetic fragrances. She threaded her way through the denimed, tattooed crowd. You're invisible, she told herself. Enveloped in the cloak of middle age.

Karla stepped closer to the auditorium, which was separated from the lobby by a ledge topped by a glass wall. She had read that the TLA held about a thousand people. Judging from the number of seats already filled in the auditorium, she figured there wouldn't be many seats open by the time the concert started. Most of the people were likely there to see the Dinosaurs, a popular hip-hop-blues group whose music was played so often on the radio that even she was familiar with it. But if even a quarter of the people there had come to see Phoebe, her daughter might have been telling the truth when she said she was on the cusp of a breakthrough.

Karla tried moving into the auditorium to get out of the mob scene but found herself blocked by a crowd clustered around the Dinosaur merchandise table. Then again, she thought, Phoebe had been poised on the cusp for the past eight years, since she'd graduated from Berklee. Why would tonight be any different?

She spotted a sign for the lady's room at the far end of the lobby. Longing for a moment's relief from the noise, she pushed her way through the crowd and into the bathroom, where a line snaked parallel to the sinks toward the stalls. The girl ahead of her turned, her heavily made-up eyes widening when they landed on her. She looked to be fourteen or fifteen and had obviously been expecting to see someone closer to her own age than to her mother's.

"You must be here to see Phoebe-Hunter," the girl said, her voice high-pitched and excited.

Karla nodded and smiled. "So I don't look like a Dinosaurs fan?" She was glad to know her daughter's average fan was a bit closer to her own age.

The girl laughed. "How do you know them? Phoebe-Hunter, I mean."

"I'm her mother. Phoebe's mother." The words, which she'd uttered so often when Phoebe was little, felt foreign in this context.

"Oh my god! Oh my god," she cried out, turning to the girl in front of her. "This is Phoebe-Hunter's mother!" She turned back and grabbed Karla's arm. "What's it like to have her grow up in your house? To hear her sing all the time? You must be so proud. And Hunter's a hunk."

"Well, it was—"

"I'm so jealous. I wish I could be you," the girl said. Then she turned back around and rushed into a stall that had just opened up.

When Karla took her seat in the auditorium, she was still processing the girl's comments. The musical equipment on stage seemed like a lot for two people. Maybe it had already been set up for both groups. Karla had no idea how those things worked. As the lights dimmed, someone shouted, "Phoebe-Hunter, Phoebe-Hunter," and a few people in the audience joined the chant. Karla's heart raced, powered by the muscle memory of concerts past, of the moments before the musicians appeared on stage. She almost forgot that it was her daughter's name they were chanting. Then Phoebe strode confidently onto the stage, followed by Hunter. They were joined by a drummer and a bass player. Phoebe planted herself center stage like a rock-blues goddess, wearing brown boots and a pink and lavender peasant dress that seemed to set her red hair ablaze. She exuded a confidence Karla had never seen in her—or perhaps had ignored until that moment. Hunter stood next to her, guitar in hand, looking more like a brother than a boyfriend, with a mass of curly hair the same color as hers.

"Hello, Philadelphia!" Phoebe shouted.

A roar ensued.

When they played the intro to their first song, the girl next to Karla squealed, "'Danger Zone.' My favorite." A few people sang along. She could only make out scattered lines, but she got the idea. *Love is a mine field...Enter at your own risk...Danger zone is where I live...If you want my love, step over the line...You'll find me in the danger zone.* Karla couldn't mistake the electricity between Phoebe and Hunter. No one would mistake them for brother and sister. Judging from the body chemistry, theirs was a category-five relationship.

It was a short set. They sang about love, grabbing onto life, and taking chances. Karla watched, entranced. Phoebe-Hunter might make it big one day; they might not. But at least, unlike Karla's dream of trying to become an astronaut, Phoebe was trying to achieve her dream with all she had.

"We'd like to end with a song we just wrote," Phoebe said. "It's called 'Flightless Bird,' and this is the first time we've played it in public. Hope you like it."

The intro was a series of chords that began in a minor key and ended in a major. It was the song Karla had heard Phoebe working on, the night she'd attempted and failed to make peace. Next came a light guitar accompaniment behind the vocals, so Karla could hear all the words. They told the story of a bird that dreamed of flying but had never learned how. Abandoned by his parents, he lived on a deserted island and had never seen birds in flight. Yet whenever the wind teased the tops of the trees and the clouds rolled by, he wanted to soar, to see what lay beyond his tiny island. One day he hopped up onto a tree branch, and then onto a higher one.

At the end of the first verse, the slow, minor-key part, Phoebe went silent and closed her eyes, as if receiving transmissions from some distant planet. At that moment, anything was possible. Then she opened her eyes and belted out the first line of the chorus a cappella. It was a plea for the bird to take a chance, to spread its wings and... She barely breathed the last word. *Fly.*

The concert hall was silent. Then Hunter joined in, followed by the drums and bass and a few people in the audience. More people sang along as they repeated the chorus. Karla found herself standing up, along with most everyone else in the theater. How had her daughter done that? She looked at the people around her as they sang, "Fly, fly." They were like congregants at a revival meeting, a flock transfigured by her daughter's full-throated preaching of the gospel of rock and freedom.

There was love in their eyes. Love for her daughter. Many of the people in the room would remember that night the rest of their lives.

Afterwards, Karla went backstage. Phoebe and Hunter were surrounded by a crowd of excited fans, and Karla couldn't get close. *Let her have her moment.* As she backed toward the exit, though, Phoebe looked up, and for a moment they were a universe of two. Karla mouthed, "Later."

She took the long way home, driving the back roads from Center City to their suburban neighborhood. At the nature preserve a couple of miles from home, she pulled into the lot and parked in front of the adjacent meadow. She got out of the car and looked up at a celebration of stars, ignoring the cool breeze that had bothered her earlier. She felt weightless, untethered, as she raised her arms to embrace them all: Cassiopeia, Orion, the Dipper, the Pleiades, the bears, the other constellations whose names she'd known since childhood. They were all there, dancing to music she was finally able to hear.

Finding Her Voice

C laire remembered the exact moment she decided to stop talking. It was on her thirtieth birthday. The family was seated around the dining room table, discussing the economy. Voices rising and falling, arms waving, silverware clinking. The entire room was in motion—except Claire, who sat like a rock in a stream as voices flowed around her. It was all so predictable, she could have scripted it.

"Money, blah, blah, profits—" The resonant baritone of her brother, the tax lawyer, commanded attention.

Enough already, she thought. This is a dining room, not a courtroom.

"Taxes, deregulation ..."

Give me a break, she continued internally. Someone should regulate that mouth and those lawyer lips. Can't someone please make him shut up. *Please. Shut. Up.* But boring as he was, they let him continue. When he was finished, his mother jumped in with the crystalline delivery of the opera singer she'd been, in a voice so striking that one had to resist the urge to demand an encore. She talked about an absolutely marvelous show they'd just seen. Then her father weighed in, echoing what her mother had just said, with his Tom Waits growl that grated on her nerves. Finally, her sister went on about something or another, her intonation rising at the end of each sentence as if every statement was a question.

Bolstered by an extra glass of wine, and a mental runthrough of what she was going to say, Claire finally plunged in, describing a fantastic book she'd just read. But she'd barely completed a sentence when her brother interrupted to ask if someone would please pass the salt. Then her mother, turning her back on Claire, asked if anyone wanted more mashed potatoes, and she gave up trying to speak. The conversation drifted downstream to another topic, making her points no longer relevant. This is how it must feel to be shot by a ray gun in an old science fiction movie, she thought. The kind that turns you transparent before it vaporizes you.

For thirty years, Claire had struggled to be heard in her family. Invariably, someone—almost always her mother—cut her off mid-sentence. Her family members made half-hearted attempts to listen when she called them out on this. But something felt different this time. A tectonic plate shifted in her core. Enough was enough. It was time to shut up for good. So shut up she did, while everyone else talked, sang "Happy Birthday," and watched Claire blow out the candles. As she had suspected, no one noticed her silence.

Later that night, Claire had second thoughts about the practicality of total silence. If she needed to communicate for urgent reasons, she'd have to gesture furiously like a mime or write messages on notepads, and people might mistake her for, say, Harpo Marx's love child. So, she decided she wouldn't completely renounce speech. Instead, she would open her mouth only when absolutely necessary. Her plan wouldn't be too difficult to carry out in terms of her career. A fact checker for a publishing house, she mostly worked at home. Claire spent the next day mapping out her strategy of silence. She would withdraw from the book club, the Bible study group, from anything that required face-to-face meetings, apart from the twice a month when she had to go into the office. Participating in group discussions had always been painful for her. Even in elementary school, Claire had rarely raised her hand—and then only after rehearsing her answer. She'd thought everyone experienced the same anxiety when speaking in groups until an extroverted friend told her how she'd always volunteered to answer questions in class and was never embarrassed when she gave the wrong answer. Claire envied her friend's weightless relationship with the world.

Claire had few friends by the age of thirty, and those that remained were scattered around the country. They kept in touch mostly by email. Even before her vow to speak as little as possible, when a friend phoned her, Claire orchestrated the conversation so they'd do most of the talking. "So the jerk actually dumped you. Wanna vent?" "How'd you end up in Des Moines, of all places?" "The wedding? Tell me everything." Now, she decided, she might not even answer the phone.

Eliminating everyday conversation would be more of a challenge. Before this decision to remain mute, Claire had constantly studied others, trying to learn the trick to interpersonal communication. At the beauty salon, she'd watched other women talk effortlessly with the hairdressers. She tried using the same topics as other clients, but her attempts fell flat. She wondered what was wrong with her. Awkwardness? Tone of voice? Was it the disconnect between the conversation she was having and the one she was trying to have, causing her to periodically stumble over words? Or was she just boring? Some essential element was missing, as if she had been absent from school the day they taught the "How to Have Normal Conversations" lesson.

Damned exhausting, all that talking. Shutting up would be a blessed relief. She'd strip all conversations to bare essentials. Why not script her responses by writing them on three-by-five cards, one card for each social situation: supermarket, subway, doctor's office. She would practice her questions and responses in front of the mirror until she could deliver them with conviction. And whenever she encountered an unanticipated situation, she'd write up a new three-by-five and study it, like a tourist using a phrase book. She felt like a tourist, always groping for the right phrase, performing silent rehearsals before speaking, as if she were translating into an unfamiliar language.

With practice, she might eventually appear normal most of the time. "How much do I owe you?" "Is that seat taken?" "D'ya have any lamb chops?"

And then there were the singing lessons. Was singing the same as speaking? If so, she'd have to stop the lessons or make radical changes to the process. No, she loved those lessons too much to give them up. And she never had trouble expressing herself through music.

She worried that she might be crossing the line between eccentricity and the nut house. But she couldn't spend the next thirty years allowing her nerves to wear her ego down to the size of a pumpkin seed.

The next day, standing in her kitchen after a quick breakfast, Claire anticipated the challenges of her first day of qualified silence. It should be a relatively easy day, she thought. A trip to the market. To the doctor.

She'd have to use public transportation to get to the doctor's office, but she had exact change, so she wouldn't have to talk to any nasty transit workers. Was abrasiveness a prerequisite for some jobs, or did employees take special classes on how to make people feel like shit? The last time she'd gone to the DMV, a battered wood counter separated the employees from the public, with the floor behind the counter higher than in front. Staring up Alice-in-Wonderland-like at one of the clerks, Claire asked for instructions, and the woman barked, "Can't you read? Sign says take a number and get in line." Then she turned to her companion and stage whispered something about stupidity.

Claire imagined taking a hammer to the big sign, laughing as shards of glass bloodied their heads. That would wipe the smirks off their smug, bureaucratic faces. But instead she said nothing, quietly turned away, and took a number. Recalling this made her realize she'd need a separate set of note cards for dealing with government workers and schmucks. These cards could include physical cues—maybe even pictures—along with scripted responses to counteract the intimidation factor. "Never lower your eyes. Never look away, dammit. Speak up." And with that thought, she headed out.

Nothing went as anticipated. At the supermarket, she had to repeat her question about where to find the breadcrumbs before the stock clerk turned around. The plus-size lady ahead of her in the express-checkout line was five items over the limit, and Claire had to restrain herself from talking. She imagined hiring some rude government worker to do the talking for her. "Look, why don't you lose those five bags of Cheetos, and while you're at it, lose about fifty pounds." Whaddya know, thought Claire, I could write a script for those nasty employees.

Claire had to wait over an hour for the doctor. He didn't bother to apologize, and he interrupted her when she tried to talk about the low-grade headaches that had plagued her since adolescence. "It's just a part of your cycle," he said dismissively, typing on his laptop. When she talked about the anxiety she'd been feeling lately, he didn't respond. Just tapped away. She had wanted to ask him for a prescription to calm her nerves, but by then his obvious irritation with either what she was saying or the way she was saying it completely shut her down. If only she could use some of the techniques she was learning from her singing teacher to help her speak up. What would happen if she sang her lines? "Doctor, I'd like some Valium" to the tune of *La Ci Darem la Mano*. Silently she mouthed the words in the direction of the doctor's bent head. Or to *Beethoven's Fifth*, "Give me some drugs. I want them now." She pictured his face, frozen, silently debating whether to prescribe a tranquilizer or have her committed.

Then she imagined holding up a card she had not yet written: Neanderthal. She chuckled, and the doctor finally looked up.

Claire climbed the steps to the second-floor studio and gave her singing teacher a hug. A small woman, Gina Carlotti had a big voice and even bigger personality. There was something about Gina that dared you not to hug her. Her favorite role was the Queen of the Night in Mozart's *Magic Flute*, which she had sung in her native Italy. "The drama of that aria—'The vengeance of hell boils in my heart'—it's a diva's dream. I could sing higher than anyone, and every time I hit that high F, *Dio mio!* The opera house exploded." Claire's lesson with Gina was the highlight of her week. She'd begun the lessons hoping to uncover a voice as powerful as her mother's, but so far, she'd found only a modest soprano.

Gina was a striking woman in her mid-fifties, with long, dark hair just turning to gray. Some days, like today, she wore it pulled straight back in a thick braid, and sometimes she let it hang loose. Claire loved the twisted pattern of the braid, gray and black intertwined. The weight of it, the *thunk* it made against solid objects when Gina turned her head quickly. Claire had never met another woman who defied the unwritten rule of short hair after menopause.

They began the lesson, as usual, with vocal exercises. Gina sat at the piano, guiding Claire's voice up and down the scales, commenting in Italian-laced English, and waving her arms, her gauzy green skirt and blouse rippling across her body. "That F sharp was muddy. Focus your voice like a pinpoint. Move the sound forward. There! Just in front of your forehead. *Ancora una volta.*"

A couple of light Italian arias followed. "Expand your diaphragm," Gina said. "Support with your pelvis. Butt in."

Claire's practice had started paying off, and sometimes she hit notes that earned a *bellisimo*, but she couldn't seem to pull it all together.

"I hear tension in your voice, *tesoro*. Relax your jaw," Gina said. "You look like a frozen popsicle." But then Claire seemed tentative, thinking about all these things she was supposed to do, and Gina said, "Don't think so hard or your brain will explode. Just open your mouth and sing."

Spesso. Addesso. Andiamo. Claire loved the velvety feel of the words. But in her struggle to master technique, she often ignored the meaning of the words she sang. She knew that great singers—singers like her mother—used their vocal gifts to tell stories.

"Where's your emotion?" Gina prodded. "Making pretty sounds? That's just musical masturbation. Sing from the heart. Make love to the audience!"

Gina ended their lesson as she ended every lesson. "You've got a voice," she said. "Use it."

These were the words Claire carried down the steps and out into the street, but they were soon drowned out by louder voices.

Claire spent the first few weeks after her birthday fine-tuning her abridged relationship with the world. Books became her new best friends—on the bus, standing in line—wherever she needed a prop to avoid conversation. It took some practice to ignore everyone she might be called upon to speak to. At the hairdresser, snippets of conversation slipped through her wall of concentration. Just got back from Aruba. Greatest movie last night. Shorter in the front this time. Whenever this happened, she refocused like a Zen master on the pages of her book.

She used the same focus to prepare for her biweekly meeting with her boss. Walking the last couple of blocks to the office, she clutched her cards in one hand and held her cell phone to her ear in the other, so she wouldn't look crazy as she practiced her lines. Each week, she customized questions for each colleague. For Mary: "Did Danny get into Saint Mark's Montessori?" For Alice: "Are you and Sam going with the destination wedding?" Quick getaway lines were a must. "Lost track of time. Gotta run." Her life had become one long rehearsal.

As the weeks passed, the world around her began losing color. She'd soon be living inside a black-and-white photo. The one swatch of color in her life was the music studio, where someone actually listened to her, believed in her, dared her to take risks.

One day toward the end of a lesson, Gina said, "I'd like you to sing something you know. Anything. Just pick a song and sing it."

"I have no idea what to sing, Gina." Claire riffled through the music she was holding. "Isn't our time up?"

Gina stood up from the piano bench and moved close to Claire, blocking her escape. "Excuses? *No.* And no using the music sheets. I won't let you leave until you sing something that's yours."

Mine, something mine. Claire's head filled with musical detritus. Eighth and quarter notes tangled in G clefs, like twisted wire hangers in a closet. Scraps of melody: Midnight, all alone in the moonlight; Fish are jumpin' and the cotton is high; Stand by your man. Her brain was concocting a music stew.

"I can't, Gina. I have to look at the words."

"Relax, *tesoro*. It will come. Everyone has a song."

Claire closed her eyes and took a deep breath. Opened her mouth. "Sometimes I feel like a motherless child. Sometimes I feel like a motherless child. Sometimes I feel like a motherless child. A long way from home. A long way from home." Her voice was a velvety contralto. The words of the old spiritual tasted like honey but cut into her heart like a knife.

Gina fixed her gaze on Claire's face. "Where were you just now, *cara*? Where did that come from?"

"I sang that in choir."

"No, where inside you did it come from?"

"I don't know," she said, while thinking: Sometimes I *do* feel like a motherless child. Claire felt like a weight had been lifted, as if she'd just gone to confession.

"Well, dig and maybe you'll find it again. This is what I want from you."

Claire was thrilled. But outside in the real world of cracked sidewalks and potholes, Claire couldn't resurrect what had happened in the studio. She kept using the note cards. Maybe with practice, she could eventually own the words she spoke, delivering them from the heart and not the script. Sure, she thought, and fish can learn to tango.

Over the next couple of months, Claire tried to meld the confidence she felt in the music studio into her everyday life, but it seemed that her self-assurance depended on a musical accompaniment. Today, Claire was headed to her voice lesson after a month-long absence while Gina visited family back in Italy.

Cards in hand, Claire settled into the long bus ride. She didn't need to use cards during the lesson, but she liked to have them handy for before and after, even though she knew most of them by heart. There were only a couple she hadn't used yet, but maybe she'd pull them out at the next family gathering: "Please shut up while I'm talking," and "Mom, why do you dismiss me?"

The seat next to her was empty, so she didn't need to use her book to stave off bus talk. Instead, she studied reflections of passengers in the soot-spattered windows and invented imaginary lives for them.

Two investment-banking guys in dark suits were huddled over a set of graphs. But maybe they were just disguised as bankers. Maybe they were on a date, deciding which hotel to go to and imagining ways to combine sex with pie charts.

A young couple in tattered jeans and T-shirts was pasted together in the back seat. His arm encircled her waist and his hand was an inch from her right breast. She didn't have to imagine what they were thinking.

She turned her attention to an elderly woman on the bench facing the aisle. Her flowered, high-necked housedress could barely contain her bulk. Wreathed in tubes of flesh, she reminded Claire of the Michelin Man. One hand rested on the handbag next to her on the seat and the other on a Bible that was open in her lap. Her life-weary eyes surveyed the passengers as her flesh undulated with the movement of the bus. Claire could imagine her internal commentary when she spied the young couple. "Wasn't like this back in the day. Women covered up. I don't wanna see other people's nasty bellies." Or maybe she was just thinking about Jesus.

The bus stopped in front of the high school and let on three rough-looking guys. One was string-bean tall; another was medium height, with bad skin. The third was a fireplug—short, thick. Their body language roared, "We own this bus now." In an odd choreography, passengers instinctively clutched their possessions tighter. Claire tightened her grip on the cards. As they closed in on the Michelin-Man lady, the rest of the riders played dumb. Looked away. Claire's gaze fixed on a knife handle sticking out of Stringbean's back pocket.

With a laugh, Fireplug bumped into the woman. No one said a thing. Claire couldn't believe they were all going to let this happen. Fireplug had his hand on the woman's pocketbook. Claire was rigid with fear. Then, out of nowhere came the rage. She forgot about the people in her life who dissed her. She forgot about the cards in her hand, the responses she'd scripted for every imaginable event. This scenario was not in the cards.

Claire stood up and tried to yell, "Stop," but the word was glue in her throat. Stringbastard pushed the woman in the face and grabbed her handbag. Claire yelled again, but all that came

out was a weak wind. *You've got a voice, use it.* Claire clutched her
cards, took a deep Gina-breath, and screamed, "Stop!" over
and over, her voice reverberating against the walls of the bus,
jolting passengers into action and exploding through an open
window. The passengers charged the three young men, but
Claire couldn't stop screaming. Swinging the stolen handbag
against the impromptu infantry, Stringbean tried to fight his
way off the bus. On his way past Claire, he stopped—revenge
trumping flight. He aimed his fist at her face, bellowing, "Shut
up, bitch!" But as the bus jolted to a stop, he missed his target and punched her full throttle in the neck. Suddenly silent,
Claire dropped her cards and clutched her throat as her attacker grabbed for his knife. She raised one of her arms to stave off
his attack and felt a sting on her forearm. Before the thug's arm
completed its downward arc to Claire's chest, one of the bankers grabbed his wrist from behind. The two of them struggled,
and the banker managed to knock the knife out of the attacker's
hand and pin him against the side of the bus. Claire watched as
a splatter of blood tattooed the cards that had spilled into the
aisle.

Hand against her throat, Claire whimpered wordlessly. She
was vaguely aware of passengers pausing to stare at her as if
she were a traffic accident before getting off the bus, and she
heard fragments of sound. Someone calling 911. A man mut-
tering, "Pays to keep your mouth shut."

The banker held the punk at bay as exiting passengers
made way for the two cops striding up the bus steps. Calmed by
the comforting blue uniforms, Claire closed her eyes. A click of
cuffs, some shit-man, take-your-hands-off-me attitude, a deci-
sive "Shut up." Heavy footsteps down the bus steps, followed by
some whistles and clapping outside. Passengers? Bystanders?
Were they cheering for the good guys or the bad?

"Everything will be all right," someone whispered in a soft
purr. Claire opened her eyes to find the fat woman about to
lay a surprisingly delicate and unblemished hand on her forehead. She continued to murmur soothingly as she wrapped

a handkerchief tightly around Claire's forearm. The white cloth quickly turned red. Some of the passengers stood nearby, watching. Claire wanted someone to pick up her cards, but with the injury to her throat, all she could utter were disjointed syllables. "What's she sayin' about cars?" one of the passengers asked. "Maybe she's got PTSD."

By the time the EMS team arrived, Claire's anguish at the possibility of losing her cards had anesthetized her to the pain, sirens, crowds. Her world had contracted into a pile of cards scattered on the floor. Not that she couldn't make another set, but these were the ones she'd worked so hard on. Pointing and grunting as the technicians lifted her onto the stretcher, she finally made herself understood.

Placing the cards on the stretcher next to her, a young paramedic remarked, "Miss, this must be some hell of a research paper you're working on." As they lifted the stretcher, she turned her head and saw a single tattered card lying in the aisle. An amputation, she thought.

The ER was beeping and buzzing as doctors cleaned out the wound on her arm and stitched it up. They poked around her mouth and inside her throat and told her they didn't think the damage was permanent, but she needed tests to be sure. Rendered temporarily mute, Claire used the backs of her cards to write answers to their questions. Every few minutes, a different white coat pulled back the curtains with a rasp and asked her the same questions as the previous coat. Eventually, Claire had written the answers to all their questions on her cards, and all she had to do was hold them up—her meds, allergies, pain on a scale of 1 to 10. Do these people ever *talk* to each other? she wondered. Maybe everyone should come to the hospital with a set of answer cards.

She was exhausted by the time they got her settled in a room. Tapping the nurse on the arm, she held up a card. "Can I please get some sleep?" The nurse shut the door behind her.

The sound of a beeping monitor and the soft hum of voices woke her. Her family was seated in cracked plastic chairs wedged into corners of her hospital room. They were absorbed in conversation, their complexions sickly in the hospital light.

Only her mother noticed that Claire was awake. When Claire's eyes met hers, she moved to the side of the bed, hugged her, and whispered, "Honey. I was worried sick about you. The nurse says she thinks you'll have your voice back in a couple of days, but we haven't heard from the doctor. *Please, baby.*"

Claire sat motionless, the monitor amplifying her heart's rhythms. *She wants me to find my voice.* Reaching down, she picked up one of the cards next to her on the bed. "In an unexpected situation," read the card, "don't lower your eyes or turn away. Maintain a steady gaze and speak firmly, and you'll be OK."

Turning the card over, she scribbled something on the back and then handed it to her mother. Claire stared at her mother as she read the message. "Doctor says I'll be OK." They were interrupted by a nurse's aide, who reached over and set the dinner tray on the table. As the aide arranged the containers, Claire wrote something on the back of another three-by-five. The smell of starchy vegetables filled the room. When the aide left, Claire slipped the card across the tray table to her mother.

This time, Claire whispered the words as her mother read silently. "Let's talk about it over dinner."

The Pool

Mrs. Raycroff felt like crap. Last month, her next-door neighbor, seventy-five-year-old Mr. Lewis, had dropped dead while running the Philadelphia Marathon. As she stood by her kitchen windowsill, watering a plant he'd given her years ago, she teared up when she remembered what a good neighbor he'd been, trimming her hedges, shoveling her walk. A model neighbor, that is, until he married his trophy wife, and then goodbye, good deeds.

Her thoughts were interrupted by a string of obscenities riding an ear-splitting backbeat through the open window. She recognized the so-called music Mrs. Trophy liked to blast when she lounged half-naked by the pool next door. Mrs. Raycroff's eyes were dry now. Served him right, she thought, running a marathon at seventy-five just to impress a trophy wife who hadn't married him for his muscles, that's for sure.

She slammed the window shut, but the glass barrier was no match for that decibel level. In her haste to get out of the kitchen, she brushed against the refrigerator, knocking a yellowed newspaper cartoon and a smiley-face refrigerator magnet to the floor. Mrs. Raycroff picked up the cartoon and examined it frame by frame, though she could have drawn it from memory. It depicted a woman's life in six panels: as a baby, a little girl, a young woman, a middle-aged woman, a senior, and finally a hunched-back old crone saying, "Well, that sucked." Mrs. Raycroff had found it so funny when she clipped it from the local paper forty-odd years ago that she'd hung it in her cubicle at work, where it stayed until she retired at sixty-five. Next, the cartoon graced her refrigerator door. But on this day, ten years later, she was suddenly at a loss to see the humor in it. Story of my goddamn life, she thought, crumpling the yellowed paper till it disintegrated in her hand. No wonder she felt like crap.

Mrs. Raycroff had been an administrative assistant for thirty-five years, and all the while she'd believed there was value in what she did. She was responsible for keeping her boss's life organized. If not for her, he often told her, his office would be in shambles. He would never have been able to find an important receipt or tax return without her. In hindsight, she realized she'd been doing little more than filing papers that went into folders that went into cabinets that went into closets no one opened. And then there was the retirement party, where her co-workers said they'd never forget her. Had any of them ever gotten in touch? A bunch of phonies. Just last week, while she was cleaning out a closet, she found a photo of that party and discovered they'd misspelled her name on the cake. A half-baked ending to a half-assed job. The photo had ended up in shreds in the trash, a fate it would now share with that damned cartoon. She put her foot down hard on the trash-can pedal to open the lid, tossed in the paper, and let the lid slam shut with a satisfying clang. Good riddance to bad rubbish, as her mother used to say.

Fuck...bitch...pimpin...homie...ho.

Those were the only words she could make out. She didn't know what those last two words meant, but they had to be something disgusting. Mrs. Trophy, a native of white suburbia, was thumbing her nose at the neighbors. Thumbing her nose at *her*. Mrs. Raycroff raised a finger that was not her thumb in the direction of the window. That felt good — so good she did it again.

Mrs. Raycroff had never acted the hussy like Mrs. Trophy did, even when she was in her prime. Even when she was in her early fifties, married, and still looking good. Even when Mr. Lewis, who was single at the time, would watch her as she bent down to pick up the newspaper or water the plants. She remembered how he'd lean over the hedges to tell her she'd be a knockout if she let her hair down and wore something colorful. And one afternoon, when she'd found herself alone with him at a neighborhood picnic, he'd pinched her backside. She'd often wondered what life would have been like with such a man, who put his hand on her body and told her she could be a knockout.

Her late husband had been affectionate enough early on, but he'd soon lost interest in putting his hands on her body, turning his attention to his real passion: whittling. Mrs. Raycroff walked into the living room and picked up a wooden owl he'd carved. His tchotchkes still covered every surface of the house, though he'd been dead almost ten years. She ran a hand over the wooden carving and cried out when a splinter pierced her palm. The sliver was long enough for her to pull out easily, but the whole exercise got her wondering why they'd married each other in the first place. Probably because they'd both been hungry: she, for companionship, and he, for chicken pot pie. She'd fulfilled her end of the implicit bargain by cooking delicious meals for him, but he was soon devoting all his waking hours to whittling perfectly good pieces of wood into perfectly ridiculous pieces of crap. Hundreds of little elves and trolls and Mickey Mouses.

Tomorrow I'll do something about this mess, she thought. But the *"fuck...bitch"* refrain next door got her blood boiling. She had to do something now. So she dragged a large carton up from the basement and swept every last one of his creations into it. *Little corpses in an open casket. Time to bury them.* She put on her gardening hat and went outside. Then she found a spade in the shed and began digging a hole in an empty section of her vegetable garden. The soil had been loosened from years of tilling, but the effort was still too much for her seventy-five-year-old body. She leaned on her spade, wiping the sweat from her brow with the back of her hand. It was crazy to think she could do something like this on a hot, humid August afternoon. She'd finish the job the next morning, when it was cooler.

The music stopped. Blessed silence. Mrs. Trophy must have gone inside. Sure enough, the lounge chair by the pool was empty. Mrs. Raycroff stood for a moment to catch her breath before laying the spade next to the half-dug hole. Suddenly a screen door slammed, and out strode Mrs. Trophy, drink in hand, her body slick with tanning oil. Mrs. Raycroff detected a faint odor of coconut. The combination of Mrs. Trophy's sun-browned body and its coconut oil coating reminded her of Almond Joy candy bars.

Her hand tightened on the spade handle as she watched Mrs. Trophy take off her bikini top and stretch out on her chair. All that grease, she thought, it's a wonder she doesn't slide off the chair. Then the music started back up. *Fuck...bitch...* That was all the fuel she needed. Hope those tits burn like hell, thought Mrs. Raycroff as she plunged her spade into the soil. When she was done, she dragged out the carton of carvings and dumped them into the hole. "Rest in peace, little buggers," she muttered as she shoveled back the dirt.

Mrs. Raycroff went inside, but the thought of Mrs. Trophy continued to enrage her. Even after a thorough scrubbing in the shower, Mrs. Raycroff couldn't wash away the smell of coconut or the phantom oily residue that she swore was clinging to her skin. The awful music continued to pound in her ears, stoking her rage.

She turned on the television, but instead of watching passively as she usually did, she vented out loud. "Damn Democrats, all wimpy and wobbly, always caving to GOP demands. The last Democratic president to stand up to the Republicans was Franklin D. Roosevelt, and he couldn't even stand up. Gets me so mad I could curse. What's stopping me? Why not? Why the hell not?" She started softly and felt something loosen inside her. It felt so good to yell "Shitty ass rat fuck!" at Wolf Blitzer. She hated that guy. One of these days she'd potty-mouth Mrs. Trophy Widow next door, swimming back and forth in her late husband's pool in a bikini that barely covered her privates. She'd yell, "Fuck, bitch, pimpin, homie, ho," right in her face.

That night, she dreamt about Mr. Lewis pulling out the pins holding her hair in a bun and looking at her with longing as he told her to wear something colorful. The next day, she went out and bought a shirt at Target that had a gold flower appliqué on one of the pockets. "Why Agnes," said one of her bridge club friends later that week, "it makes you look so...shiny." Mrs. Raycroff took that as a compliment and went back the next day to buy a blouse covered with rhinestones.

Despite the new wardrobe and her newfound freedom of speech, the rage still burned. Sometimes she looked out the window and watched Mrs. Trophy as she swam or basted herself with oil, like roasting poultry, and thought, *Husband killer*! Probably sexed him up good and then sent him out to run twenty-six miles, knowing his seventy-five-year-old heart couldn't take all that stimulation.

Summer slowly gave way to fall, and Mrs. Trophy no longer swam in her pool, but Mrs. Raycroff still felt anger, now tinged with a hint of sadness and something else she couldn't identify. Then one day Mrs. Trophy carried a suitcase out to her car and took off with her boyfriend, a stocky fellow with "USDA Prime" tattooed on his back, as if he were a slab of beef. Mrs. Raycroff watched as the red sports car burned rubber and sped off into the distance. It was as if Mrs. Trophy was giving the finger to poor Mr. Lewis. Tears filled her eyes at the memory of who Mr. Lewis had once been and who she might have been.

That night, she watched the outside lights come on next door and saw the surface of the pool shimmering like her new blouse. She went outside and slipped through the gate.

Standing at the shallow end, she stared at the water. "Bitch," she said softly, then louder, then at the top of her lungs: "BITCH." The dam burst, releasing all the anger and the what-ifs and the might-have-beens into the star-filled night, leaving her diffused with joy.

Mrs. Raycroff took off her blouse and pants and tossed them on the grass. She heard applause and laughter coming from a nearby TV and yelled, "Fuck the neighbors" as she shed her underwear. A breeze ruffled the surface of the water as she took the pins out of her hair. With her shriveled skin and wild hair, she figured she must look like one of her late husband's wooden trolls. "Fuck the trolls," she said as she walked down the steps into the pool, head held high, like a bride descending a staircase. She doggie paddled before switching to the Australian crawl. Not bad for an old fart, she thought as she got into the rhythm of the strokes.

When she got tired, she doggie paddled back to the shallow end. She raised her torso, mermaid-like, out of the water, and felt the cool night air raise goose bumps on her skin. Finally, Mrs. Raycroff knew how it felt to be alive.

Tango

The year we both turned twenty, on a star-drenched night, Michael and I ran naked into the Atlantic Ocean. The water was unusually cold for August—too cold for us to do anything but hug each other in a futile attempt to keep warm. I was reluctant to pull away from his embrace, but my chattering teeth were not conducive to intimacy, so I told him I'd meet him back on the beach. I waded to shore, and he called out to me.

"Alicia."

I turned.

"You're beautiful," he said, smiling, wrapping me again in a blanket of love. "Marry me."

His proposal confirmed something we'd known since we were children, long before we'd discovered sex, or loneliness, or loss. "Yes, of course," I answered.

Ten years later, I was reminded of that night by the two photographs hanging on the wall of a therapist's waiting room. In one, three little girls were holding hands and dancing in a circle on the beach. In the other, a couple twirled on a fishing pier that jutted out into a moonlit sea. If I hadn't known the therapist's specialty, the pictures would have given it away: dance therapy.

I had come to interview Dr. Gordon for a feature article I was writing for the *San Francisco Chronicle* on unconventional therapies. I was thinking about an introduction to the article when he opened the door to his office and invited me in.

Dr. Gordon was tall and angular, with crystalline blue eyes, a generous smile, and a full head of white hair, though with his unlined skin he couldn't have been older than forty.

"People come to me because they like the idea of dancing," he explained after I'd settled into the couch facing his chair, "but they're often uncomfortable the first time they're actually in the studio. So, we talk first."

"I can understand that."

"But since we don't have the luxury of time, I'd like to start off in the studio so you can get a feel for the process. I find that my patients express their feelings better in my office after they've expressed them in the studio."

He led me into the dance studio, an intimidating expanse of hardwood floor and mirrors. "Why don't we start with some stretches and then a little free movement?"

I turned my head to avoid looking directly into the floor-to-ceiling mirror. Maybe I was avoiding the mirror because the hairdresser had just cut my red, curly hair too short, like Little Orphan Annie's. Or it could have been the discrepancy between the image I had in my head and the one that would face me in the mirror.

"That's okay," he said, noticing my body language. "A lot of people are uncomfortable looking at themselves at first."

I turned to face the side wall, and he led me through a series of head rolls, shoulder shrugs, and arm stretches. Then he put on some Middle Eastern music and told me to close my eyes and move with the music. I was there to write an article about this kind of therapy, so I did what he asked, but I hoped he wasn't looking. In a few minutes, he turned off the music, and I opened my eyes with relief.

I followed him into his office and sat back down on the couch.

"This therapy is all about the relationship between emotion and movement," he said. He stretched his legs forward and crossed his feet at the ankles. His legs seemed to go on forever. "How did you feel in there?"

"Awkward."

He nodded. "I tell my patients that we hold the truth in our bodies."

"Truth is, I'm a klutz," I said, telling more than I'd intended to. "My husband and I took dance lessons before our wedding so we wouldn't embarrass ourselves. He took to the lessons, but I was pretty hopeless. Still am, after ten years of marriage."

He laughed. I took out my notebook and began asking him questions. As he answered, I found myself subconsciously imitating his movements—crossing my legs at the ankles, straightening my shoulders. Who was I kidding? Though blessed with the long, lean body of a dancer, I was anything but.

As he walked me out, he said, "With time, I could teach you to loosen up."

I smiled. "That would make you a miracle worker."

"I'm loving this assignment," I said to Michael's back as he went through the mail that evening. The sun had lost its daily battle with the San Francisco fog, leaving blood-red streaks in the sky as it descended. Outer Sunset was one of the foggiest districts in the city, so such a glorious sunset was all the more precious for its infrequency. Ours was a tract house with the merest slice of a beach view from the corner of our balcony. But the salt air and the sound of gulls made up for the obstructed view. And on clear days, the light shimmered like a Monet painting.

"Mmm," said Michael, half turning.

"Learning all the ways people can get *shrunk*. Yesterday I interviewed a sand-tray therapist. Can you believe—"

He looked at his watch. "Sorry. Got a lot of work to do before dinner. Let's talk then."

The old Michael would have said something funny, maybe conjugated the verb "to shrink." When had he stopped laughing?

We ate dinner sitting on the couch with the TV on and took our dessert out to the small table on the balcony. All that remained of the day was a brush stroke of light tracing a line between sky and sea. I asked him if he thought the cake I'd baked was good (yes), if he'd had a bad day (no), if he thought the sunset was especially beautiful (yes). That's how the dinner conversation went. Call and response. If I stopped calling, he stopped responding. His eyes were focused somewhere between the beach and infinity.

In years past, I would have told my astronomer husband he looked like he was lost in space. I would have asked about his research at the university or his visit to the local elementary school to talk about why Pluto was no longer a planet. What the hell, I thought. Let's give it one more try.

"The sand in that tray yesterday reminded me of New Jersey sand."

"Tray?"

"The one I mentioned before dinner. At the sand-tray therapist's office."

He gave a distracted nod.

"Reminded me of all those summers we spent next door to each other down the shore. Know what my first memory was?" I was talking faster and louder, trying to hold his attention. "I thought of the tin can and string telephones we used to stretch between our two houses. Remember how we'd send messages to each other at night? Made faces until our parents made us turn out the lights?"

He smiled, and I caught a glimpse of the boy who'd evolved from best friend to lover to life partner. But too soon, his mouth straightened to its default shape. I wanted to weep.

I'm a writer, I thought. I know words, know how to string

them together to create stories that move people. Why can't I come up with the right words to move him? Maybe he would have been more interested in the dance therapist. He, unlike me, could dance.

Driving home from work the next day, as the sun passed behind a cloud, I remembered when Michael had stopped laughing. It was after his father's death a year earlier. Michael and his father hadn't been close—we'd only seen him a handful of times since our wedding. He'd told me about his father's passing casually, like he'd have mentioned the death of a classmate he hadn't thought about in years. Dr. Markowitz had been a presence in our summer lives—magnetic, dark, handsome. Women had certainly taken notice. Michael vaguely resembled his father— long legs, brown-black hair—but what Michael lacked in magnetism he used to make up for in warmth. I thought back on all the summers we spent next door to them and realized I never saw Dr. Markowitz hug his son.

I tried to get him to talk about their relationship when he told me his father had died. I believed that children always mourn the loss of a parent, regardless of the distance between them. But I felt as if I were flipping through pages of a photo album in which someone had cut a father-shaped slice out of each picture.

"How did you *feel*, when you heard the news?" I'd asked.

"Why are you asking me all this now?"

Why now, he asks? Like this isn't the first time I've tried to get through to him about his father. About whatever it was that was shutting him down. "Because it's time for you to talk."

"He's not worth talking about. We weren't close. I don't miss him. Full stop."

The day after I visited the dance therapist, Michael sat at the breakfast table, books and papers spread out before him, while I was sprawled on the floor, trying to write the final draft of my article. The silence had become unbearable and I couldn't concentrate.

"Michael, we need to talk."

"About what?"

"Us."

"What about us?"

Everything about us. "I don't know." I got up from the floor and sat down at the table across from him. "Things have changed."

"What things?"

"Such as, you're not interested in hearing about my work anymore."

"Well you're not interested in hearing about mine, either."

"That's not true. I'm interested, but you're not talking." I reached out and touched his upper arm. He brushed it off.

"Christ, Alicia. What do you want from me?"

"I want...I want...tango lessons."

"Tango?" He looked as astonished as I felt by my answer.

"Yes. I want you to dance with me."

Señor Robles looked like the tango instructor he was. Licorice-black, slick hair, thin mustache, slim hips accentuated by tight pants. No surprise there. It was Michael who surprised me. He'd always been coordinated, but I couldn't get over how quickly he took to the complicated tango rhythm. He instinctively knew how to hold his body, turn, lead me in the right direction. I don't know why I'd chosen tango. I'd have had an easier time with cha-cha or box step. When you have a lousy sense of direction, you should steer clear of dances where there are so many unexpected turns that you never end up where you expected. Maybe it was the posters I'd seen around town of the Tango Flame Dancers that had captured me, their bodies pressed together as if glued.

"Keep your back straight, like Miguel," Señor Robles would remind me. "Lean back, Alicia. Trust your partner. He won't let you fall. Look into his eyes when he brings you close. In that moment there are no secrets between you." He spoke like a character in an old black-and-white movie from the thirties. We looked at each other as instructed, but it still felt as if we were two strangers dancing together.

Señor Robles told us to practice at home and gave us records of the music he used during our lessons. I had to nag Michael to practice with me, but once we started dancing, he participated without complaint, maneuvering me through the moves. Once, when we were practicing and all the moves were going right, I imagined someone looking in our window, jealous of the intimacy on display. But the truth was, even when we were pressed close as lovers, our talk was all business. "Turn, turn, lean." "No, Alicia, go left." It was no different than when we weren't dancing. But the dancing brought us closer—if only in the physical sense—which was better than nothing.

Señor Robles was right when he said anyone could master basic tango with enough practice. Even me. As some of the steps became automatic, he had us concentrate on attitude. "You dance tango with the feet, yes, but also with the eyes." He'd reach over to adjust the placement of a hand or tilt of the head. "Passion, indifference, disdain, passion again—that is the face of seduction. Look deep into his eyes, Alicia, as he pulls you close."

I did as I was told and saw…nothing. Or was I missing something?

"Now turn away," said Señor Robles, and once again I did as I was told.

At times I was sorry I'd insisted on dance lessons instead of dance therapy with Michael. My patients express their feelings better in my office after they've expressed them in the studio, Dr. Gordon had said. That wasn't happening here. We were becoming better dance partners, attuned to the subtlest gestures. A light touch on the shoulder was a signal for me to turn; his palm pressed against the small of my back meant he was about to bend me backward. But that did not make us better life partners.

Señor Robles gave us a DVD of Tango Flame to inspire us. "Watch," he ordered. "Then practice. Repeat, repeat, again, again. The message of the dance is passion, but you can't show passion until you've mastered technique."

I wished there were a technique I could master that would bring back the passion.

But even after we'd mastered the dance moves, there was no real passion between us. I realized that nothing was going to change. We'd go on living our split lives, one where we danced and one where we did everything else. That August we even missed the Perseid meteor shower, something we'd watched together every August since we were kids. We used to stretch out on beach blankets and scan the skies. *Did you see that one? Look over there above the pier. Oh, wow.* We hadn't even missed it when we'd gone off to different colleges. Every year we'd reunite to watch those streaks of light shoot like flaming bullets from a celestial firing range. I suspected that my astronomer husband hadn't forgotten the Perseids; he'd simply decided it wasn't important for him to celebrate them with me anymore.

When we weren't working late, Michael and I watched television, God's gift to dysfunctional couples. It didn't much matter what we watched. We sat on the sofa with a bowl of pop-corn or chips between us, touching only accidentally when we reached into the bowl at the same time. We went to bed at different times, so the touching there was accidental as well.

A few months after my article was published, we were watching something on TV with a twisty plot. Unable to follow it, I gave up and thought about my upcoming lunch meeting with Dr. Gordon. He'd called me earlier that day to tell me how much he'd loved the article and invited me out to lunch to thank me in person for all the new client calls he'd been getting ever since. I imagined how our lunch would go. He'd ask me to call him Robert, and after lunch, he'd give me a dance lesson at his studio. *You're good, Alicia,* he'd say. *Let me show you how to relax.* And I'd tell him how my life was not as I had expected. He'd tell me of his own lost dreams. Equally unburdened, we'd do the tango. Our feet would barely skim the hardwood floor.

I didn't notice when Michael got up from the sofa, so when I heard the intro to "El Dia Que Me Quieras," I thought it was TV background music. But then I felt his hand under my arm, pulling me up roughly. When he fitted my body to his, I could feel his tension. We got to the part of the dance where he was supposed to push me away, but instead he gripped my arm and locked me to him. The unexpected forcefulness of the move scared me.

"There was this kid came up to me after I gave my astronomy talk to his class," he whispered in my ear. He had to bend awkwardly to reach my ear, since he was so much taller, but we kept dancing. "A second grader with a bowl haircut. Latched onto me, arms around my waist, and said he wanted to be an astronomer just like me. Then he said something else. I couldn't make it all out, but I think he said he wished I was his father." The music ended. "I know that little boy, Alicia. I know him."

"Yes, yes, I understand," I lied soothingly, waiting for him to go on. But he had nothing more to say.

I arrived early at the little restaurant in the Haight. Dr. Gordon was already there, tall and poised at the round table. During lunch he told me how he'd studied ballet and then switched to modern. He'd broken his ankle when he was thirty, so he'd gone back to school and gotten a Ph.D. in psychology. I told him about my family on the East Coast, our summers at the shore, and the excitement of working for big-city newspapers. I didn't talk about my relationship with Michael or about tango, but he was a psychologist, so he may have intuited that I wasn't happy. I told him I might want to schedule an appointment with him to discuss some of my "issues." He said he'd be happy to listen.

As we finished our coffee, his leg brushed mine. It might have been accidental—him arranging his dancer's legs—but it might not have been. I hadn't thought about another man that way since before I got married. I was sure Michael was all I needed. At some level I was still sure, but there I was, sitting across from a man with a sympathetic voice and eyes the color of the afternoon sky. He was wearing a wedding ring. So was I. Maybe his partner's a guy, I thought, and this is all perfectly safe. I told him I'd call to set up an appointment.

That night, I caught Michael looking at me as I reached for the popcorn. "What?" I said, but he shook his head and turned back to the screen. I considered slipping him a note under his pillow. *Dear Michael. How are you? I miss you.*

Then an old friend from back East called. I knew it would be a long conversation, since we hadn't talked in a while. I picked up the landline extension in the bedroom, stretching out across the bed and hanging my feet over the edge like I had when I was a kid. We reminisced about old friends at the shore, and when she asked about Michael's parents, I told her both of them had died. "It's funny, Shelly. He talks about his mother all the time, but never about his father. It's as if he never had one."

Latin music played softly in the background, and I thought maybe Shelly had taken up tango, too. But when the music got louder, I realized it was coming from the next room, through the phone I'd forgotten to hang up when I took the call. *Como rie la vida si tus ojos negros me quieren mirar.* I told Shelly I had to go, hung up, and walked into the living room. Michael was standing by the table, his hand on the phone, which was now resting in its charger. He wasn't angry. He wasn't anything. Then he said, "Dance with me."

He held me and we swayed.

"Sometimes my father came to my room late at night," he told me. "I never told my mother. It would have killed her." His words were barely audible. "I'd wake up and there he was next to me. I didn't cry. I just went somewhere else inside until he left. I don't remember much. Just touching, I think. But I went so far away, I'm not sure."

The music pulsed, but we moved to our own rhythm, rocking from side to side. The beat was relentless, the same music from the Tango Flame dance where the man grabs the woman and pulls her close, and she tries to pull away, but he twists his leg around hers and traps her. But we just rocked, and somehow I felt closer to my husband than I ever had before, even during our most intimate moments.

The song finished and the music stopped, but we swayed in silence.

Then Michael spoke again. "That night when I proposed to you, when we dove into those waves and it was so cold and we came up and the stars were so close, I felt...I guess it's how those Jesus people feel when they've been born again. I'd been born again—without a father."

I shivered, as if plunged once again into those cold waters. We stood motionless in the silent room, his arms wrapped tightly around me, as if I were a life preserver. I wanted to soothe him with words, but I let my body comfort him instead.

He had held the truth in his body all those years. How had he kept it inside? How could I not have known why he never wanted to turn the lights out those nights at the shore when we were connected by tin cans and string? How had he learned to love with all that scar tissue around his heart?

I didn't know whether we'd ever speak about this again, or whether the dance we were doing was the only comfort he'd accept from me. But I knew I was the only person he'd ever tell, and if it hadn't been for me, the waves, the cold, and the stars, Michael would still be that lost little boy.

Not Quite As Advertised

It wasn't easy to let my car park itself the first time, but I took a leap of faith, letting go of the steering wheel and easing my foot off the brake. The Lexus backed her shiny silver butt into the space between the Prius and the Expedition, as advertised. Inheritance well spent. Thanks, Mom.

A week later, I drove to Whole Donuts for a snack. I should have walked—it's only a mile from my house, and I've picked up a few pounds since the divorce—but I was loving my new toy way too much to leave her home alone. According to the dashboard readout, there was enough room to fit into the small parking spot in front of the entrance, so I let her take control. But instead of parking, she drove past Whole Donuts and stopped at the corner. "Your route guidance is finished," she purred.

When she refused to move, I grabbed the wheel, more than a little pissed. "I guess I'll have to do this myself," I said. "Those chocolate glazed won't wait forever."

I circled the block, determined to park in front of Whole Donuts. As we glided past Vinnie's Vegan, she stopped, assumed the parallel position, parked herself, and refused to budge until I'd gotten out and bought myself a quinoa burger. Feh. I checked the owner's manual for information about doughnut-related parking malfunctions but found nothing.

After eating the pseudo-burger, I pulled a Marlborough out of the pack I'd hidden in the first-aid kit. But every time I struck a match, the A/C kicked in and blew it out. I got out of the car and had a quick smoke on the sidewalk—turning my back to the car, just to be on the safe side. When I turned around, I could have sworn I saw her raise and lower the antenna, as if giving me the finger. I returned the salute.

From then on, I made my doughnut runs on foot, and the car let me go about my business: gym, hairdresser, nail salon. In fact, I was starting to look pretty good, and my friends convinced me it was time to get out and meet some guys, so I subscribed to an online dating service. After much electronic back-and-forthing, I found Scott, a dentist who liked movies, long walks, and chocolate glazed doughnuts. We arranged to meet at a Starbucks across town.

I found a spot near the coffee shop and let the car self-park. But when I tried to get out, I discovered the doors were stuck in the locked position. I hadn't anticipated vehicular pushback; over the last few weeks, I'd come to accept my car's hostility toward fatty food and cigarettes, but what could she possibly have against my attempts to find a soul mate?

My new car was beginning to drive me crazy—kind of like my mother, who in spite of our differences never failed to steer me on the right path. The more I thought about it, as I sat there, locked in the car, the more convinced I became that my mother's spirit had gone locomotive. Maybe my car/mother knew something about the guy I was about to meet and was sending me a warning. I googled him on my smart phone, right there outside of Starbucks, and sure enough, found a picture of him alongside his lovely wife, Cathy, and his two lovely daughters, Madison and Taylor. Just like my ex-husband, Steve, who'd sworn undying love as he secretly e-harmonized himself into the arms of another woman: my best friend, Katie.

Mom had warned me not to marry him. Said he was the philandering type. "If he ever treats you wrong," she told me when we got engaged, "I promise to make his life a living hell."

I'd never taken her up on that offer. But now I was ready. "You're on, Mom," I said, patting the steering wheel. "The bastard walked out just like you said. Left me at the mercy of fast food and married men. Time to make good on your promise." I pressed the start button. "Now take me home." She burned rubber as she pulled away from the curb, as if she knew exactly what I was thinking.

When I got home, I called my ex and suggested that we exchange cars. Told him I'd feel safer with his Subaru, what with the snow and all. When he offered to pay me the difference, I graciously declined.

On the day of the exchange, I drove the car to Steve's and let her park herself one last time. "Your route guidance is finished," she purred.

"You're right, Mom," I said as I walked up the steps to his apartment, car key in hand. I would have loved my mother to continue guiding me toward a healthier life style and the perfect mate, but I figured Steve needed the guidance more than I did. I suspected my mother would not treat him kindly, and I was right.

A week later, I got the call from Steve to pick up the goddamn car.

"What happened," I asked in the most honied tones I could muster.

"What *didn't* happen?" He yelled so loud, I had to turn the volume on my phone down to the lowest setting. "Whenever I started to watch one of those … you know … adult videos, the car alarm would go off outside. Woke the whole damn neighborhood. Then, the other night during that blizzard when I went to pick up Kat...my date, the car stalled out a block from her house and my, er...date had to trek through a foot of snow to get to me. And when I finally got the car started, something shorted out underneath the seats. Shocked the hell out of our...

our ...down there. I'm not going to tell you what happened after that."

Ooo, please tell me, I thought. But I answered, "Tsk tsk."

"This is going to sound crazy, but you know how your mother despised me? It was almost as if she'd returned from the dead to make my life a living hell."

"That *is* crazy," I answered. "My mother hated cars."

The Weight Of Loss

When I walked into her apartment for the first time, Vera was wearing shorts the color of Jersey tomatoes, her massive thighs inflating the fabric like carnival balloons. She must have weighed over four hundred pounds, and if I'd seen her on the street, I'd have stared; since this was an interview, I smiled and introduced myself. She shook my hand, remaining planted in her easy chair.

"Sit," she said, pointing to a maroon loveseat. I sank into a rump-shaped crater in the center of a brocade cushion.

"I almost called the *Inquirer* to cancel," she said, "but I like your column, Alicia, so I decided to give it a go."

Vera's dark, curly hair was pulled back, exposing a moon face. She had dark eyes, olive skin, and a mouth one would describe as sensual if it hadn't been surrounded by all that flesh. I could make so much more of that mouth with lipstick. I was already starting to edit her.

Vera leaned back, resting her hands on her thighs, as I flipped my notebook open. The room was dark, with heavy curtains blocking the windows and the elaborate shades covering the Victorian lamps. I scribbled *Shut in?* and looked up.

"Why don't we get started?" I asked. "Would it be okay if I recorded our conversation?" I held up my cell phone. She looked at the notebook on my lap and nodded with raised eyebrows.

"Old habits die hard," I said with a smile, turning on the recorder before taking my pen out. "Okay. Would you like to tell me about—"

"Cookie?" She picked up a box of Chips Ahoy! from the side table.

I thanked her and took one, but she shook the box until I took another. At the sound of the rattling box, a black cat jumped from the windowsill onto the table, then onto her lap. Vera grabbed a cookie and delicately nibbled around the circumference before popping the rest of it in her mouth. She did the same with a second cookie. Eat and repeat. She chewed slowly, eyes closed, as if engaging a lover. I turned away.

My eyes had adjusted to the dim light, and I scanned the room, focusing on an arrangement of gold-framed photos mounted on a wall that was painted mustard yellow.

Swallowing the last of the cookies, Vera opened her eyes, cradling the cookie box in her arms.

"You like chartreuse?"

"That color? Yes. It's...different, nice," I lied. As a rule, I kept my distance from chartreuse, which clashed with my red hair and turned my pale skin sickly.

"My mother hated chartreuse. She was an interior designer. Went by the name of Giovanna—changed the 'i' at the end of our family name to 'a.' Ever heard of her?"

I shook my head side to side.

"Anyway, she'd die if she saw that wall, but since she's already dead, there's nothing to worry about. Died when she was forty, like all the others in my family." I jotted, *Weight problem runs in family?*

"Sorry for—"

"It happens." She rattled the box. "Another cookie?" I shook my head, and she reached into the box. Obscene, stuffing her mouth like that. Probably avoided mirrors. I knew all about that. I'd gained thirty pounds when I broke up with my first boyfriend. It took a year, but I managed to lose all the weight. If *I* could do it, anyone…

"You can write this down for your readers," she said. "We fatties get good at reading peoples' faces when they look at us. We know what they're thinking: Disgusting. How could she let herself get like that? No excuse. Fat as a pig, horse, elephant, take your pick. Tub of lard. Butterball." Her voice rose.

"That's got to be tough. How do you handle it?"

"I tried to develop a tough skin, but it seems all I developed was this." She shook a pendulous upper arm and chuckled.

I snuck a glance at my watch as I considered my looming deadline and lack of progress on the interview. *My fault for letting my own prejudice derail me.*

"Why don't I make us some tea? We can sit in there." She pointed toward the kitchen, and I nodded. "You look like the type who drinks herbal. Oh, maybe not." She looked me up and down, as if searching for clues to my hot beverage preferences. "You're the black coffee, keep-it-coming type. Isn't that what reporter types like you always drink?"

"Matter of fact—"

"I like it black, too, when I pour it from the pot." She grabbed the sides of the chair to help herself up. "But then I add plenty of cream and sugar, so it doesn't taste like shit."

I laughed, and she smiled at my reaction.

Vera didn't make it up from her chair on the first try, and as she fell back onto the cushions, her shirt pulled up to reveal an expanse of white, doughy flesh. She caught me staring and pursed her lips. In the stillness that followed, I became aware of something classical playing softly in another room.

"This isn't going to work," she said. "I know I said yes to this interview, but now…I want you to go."

"I'm sorry if I—"

"Go."

Like all the other women I'd interviewed, Vera was prickly about her weight; but she was different—funnier, feistier, open about her eating habits. If I could just hang in a little longer, maybe I'd be able to establish a rapport.

"GO!"

I got up reluctantly. "Thank you for your time."

She said nothing as I walked to the door, passing the photos on the mustard wall. They were all shots of dark-haired women bearing a vague resemblance to each other and to Vera. One photo hanging off to the side showed a boy of about nine or ten with windswept blond hair, standing in front of the LOVE statue in Center City. He held out an ice cream cone like an offering to whoever was taking the picture.

I drove to the office, replaying the disastrous interview, wondering why I could hold my own at bloody crime scenes and suicides, even conjure up a look of sympathy when interviewing a child molester—anything to get the story—but couldn't offer up a modicum of sympathy or objectivity when I looked obesity in the face.

When I got to the office, my message light was blinking. I listened. *This is Vera. Changed my mind. Give me a call.*

Back at my apartment, I settled into a comfortable chair to start the process of transforming my notes into prose. This usually came easily, but that day I couldn't concentrate. Something about the perpetual twilight of Vera's apartment, the chartreuse wall, the bulky furniture that echoed the dimensions of its owner. A far cry from our sleek, modern apartment with its freshly painted walls—all white except for the spare bedroom, which Jamie and I had agreed to keep bright yellow. Six months had passed since my last miscarriage—we'd been so sure we were finally going to have a baby. Sadly, the room was still unfurnished. Waiting. We were not ready to give up yet, but my optimism was wearing thin.

"It was her don't-give-a-damn attitude about her weight

that got to me," I told Jamie over dinner, "like she was actually proud of it. She joked about her weight, called herself a fatty, shook a box of cookies in my face like they were maracas. And she was so different from the others I interviewed— those women who never ate a crumb in front of me, all full of excuses: *I eat like a bird but keep getting fatter. I never have more than a thousand calories a day, I swear. Tried every diet. Must be my thyroid.*"

"Maybe she wants to be fat," said Jamie.

"Nobody wants to be fat."

"How can you be so sure?"

"Who would choose to be like that?"

"Maybe that's the story."

I thought I'd gotten a handle on the reasons people gained weight, but I hadn't considered the possibility of people who chose to put on the armor of obesity to protect themselves against personal demons—afflictions even scarier than Type 2 diabetes, strokes, and unrelenting condemnation.

Vera met me at her apartment door in a loose-fitting, floral-print dress that made her look like she was wearing a shower curtain. At least there'd be no unwelcome midriff exposure. I must have hidden my reaction well, because she smiled and led me down the hall to the kitchen/breakfast room. This time she sported long, black filigree earrings with tiny bells that tinkled when she moved her head.

"Coffeepot and cups on the counter. Help yourself. Cookies too, if you'd like."

The counter was lined with cookie jars, cracker boxes, and an assortment of Entenmann's cakes.

I filled a mug and sat down across from her at the kitchen table, a plate of petit-fours between us. I took out my notebook and pen.

"Fire away," she said.

"As you know, this is an article about weight gain. The rise of obesity. How and why people get...gain weight."

"It's okay to say *fat*. I've heard worse." She picked up a pastry and pointed it at me. "And we both know how people get that way, don't we?" she said with undisguised sarcasm, taking a bite. She finished it off with a lick of the fingers. *In my face.*

"But there are different paths for different people. Was yours a quick weight gain, or did it sneak up on you?"

She looked at the pastries on the table between us. "Mine was sudden onset. I can tell you exactly when I started down that path. August twenty-fifth, three years ago."

"What happened then?"

Her attention was still focused on the petit-fours, as if they held all the answers. Piano music played softly in the background, as it had during my last visit. "Something...something they told me at work." She looked over at the counter. "I went home and pulled a Sara Lee out of the freezer—one I'd been saving for company. It was a pecan coffee cake—you know, the one that's shaped like a ring with icing drizzled on top. Stuck it in the oven and pulled it out before it was totally defrosted. When I broke off a chunk, I smelled the cinnamon—nothing like cinnamon to fill your holes." She closed her eyes, saliva pooling along her lower lip. "I held that first bite in my mouth—it was too delicious to swallow—just sucked on it till it was gone. One bite and I was hooked. They should put warning labels on those boxes. I couldn't stop until I'd eaten the whole thing." She looked me straight in the eye. "Turns out Sara Lee was my gateway pastry."

I choked on my coffee, trying unsuccessfully to keep a straight face. But when she threw her head back and roared with laughter, I had to join in. At that moment she seemed to genuinely enjoy poking fun at herself, but the circumstances of her weight gain told a different story.

"So, what else do you want to know?" she asked once she'd caught her breath.

"Were you heavy as a child?"

"Maybe a little chubby, but it didn't bother me much. The guys I dated seemed to prefer women with meat on their bones. But I didn't eat like a horse back then—or look like one. In fact, an artist I was engaged to wanted to paint me as Aphrodite."

Aphrodite. She must have really been something. I asked her about her childhood eating habits and the diets she'd tried. Then I asked about her family.

"Did any of them have weight problems?"

"My family." She nodded in the direction of the living room wall. "You saw them hanging on the wall: mother, sister, aunts, grandmother. Did any of them look fat to you?"

I shook my head and waited for her to go on. The piano music in the background sounded vaguely familiar, but I didn't know much about classical music, so I couldn't put a name to it.

"Those pictures were taken when each of them was thirty-seven, thirty-eight, a year or two before they died."

"I'm so sorry. Was it genetic?"

"Not unless being cursed is genetic. My grandmother died of lung cancer, Mom had a stroke, one of my aunts had breast cancer, the other had a heart attack, and my sister...my sister was hit by a car."

I looked over at the wall. "Is your picture up there?"

"No, I only put up dead people."

No family. All dead. And the boy?

"They were all amazing. My grandmother was an attorney, and one of my great-aunts was a psychiatrist, way before the women's liberation movement. My aunt wrote novels. Remember *A Tree in the Woods*?" I nodded. "And my mother the decorator had her work featured in *Town and Country*."

"What about your sister?"

"Monica. We were fraternal twins. She was a musical genius." Her voice faded, and she looked down at her hands. "Mom told me her grandmother had died young, too, so the curse must go way back. I think that's why the Giovanni women were all so driven. Mom was only twenty when she had Monica and me. She told us that if we wanted to do great things, we'd better do them while we were young." She paused, closing her eyes. "You'll be wanting to know what I do...did. I was a social worker. Used to tell people I was in the business of saving babies. Other people's babies. Not that I didn't want kids of my own—I think I'd have been a great mother." She chuckled and seemed to lose her train of thought for a moment.

"But once I reached my late twenties, I decided it would be irresponsible to have a kid. The poor thing would be orphaned before he hit puberty. So, I saved other people's babies instead. That's what social workers do. And what's more important than that? I don't know what Mom really thought about my career, but she always said she was proud of me. I wasn't a musical genius like Monica, or artistic like Mom. But my colleagues told me I was a damned good social worker." She ate a piece of pastry she'd sequestered in her fist.

Filling holes. That's what she was doing. Holes left by people she'd lost. I filled mine with hope, and she filled hers with Entenmann's.

"That boy in the picture?"

She stiffened. "He..." She turned away from the picture wall. "Didn't you want to ask me about my health?"

"Of course." I leaned forward. "How's your health?"

"Healthy as a horse. I don't take meds, my heart's strong, and I've got the blood pressure of a runner."

"You're in better shape than I am." I smiled and leaned in toward her. "Did you ever try to lose that weight? When I gained a few pounds, I stuck a picture of a bathing suit I wanted on the fridge. Worked for me. Maybe you—"

"I studied journalism before I went into social work, so I know all about objectivity. More than I can say for my friends, who couldn't stop offering advice once I started gaining weight. 'I'll go on a diet with you.'" Her voice rose. "'Have you tried Atkins? What about the freaking grapefruit diet?' So, here's how it's going to be if you want to go on interviewing me. No more diet advice. No 'what a pretty face,' or 'thin person inside waiting to get out' shit."

A cell phone rang. She fumbled for it in the voluminous folds of her dress before quietly telling the caller her services wouldn't be needed today, the apartment was clean enough already. She reburied the phone and looked at me, head cocked like a puppy. The gypsy earrings tinkled.

"What?"

"When are you coming to see me again?"

I heard the need in her voice, and my professionalism unofficially went to hell, but I'd already interviewed enough people for the article. And though I'd said nothing to her about my miscarriages, I got the sense that she saw me as a kindred spirit—someone who had also suffered losses. Then again, it could have been my own neediness I was hearing.

By the next visit, both of us knew I was no longer coming as a journalist, though neither of us was willing to acknowledge it just yet. I still brought my notebook, but it stayed in my bag, as did the recorder.

We were all small talk until I suggested we go outside for a walk to get some fresh air.

"You're doing it again. Trying to get me to lose weight."

"Not at all. Just thought you might be feeling claustrophobic."

"I like my apartment. It's cozy. Have you ever considered that some people actually prefer staying inside? And what's with your fresh air obsession? You think it'll make me healthy?" Her voice rose, as if she were on the verge of tears. "Maybe I don't want to be healthy. Ever thought of that? Maybe I'm already too damn healthy." She was breathing heavily, testing the limits of her overstretched clothing.

"I'm forty-two years old, two years older than my sister when she died. Older than every woman in my family. Maybe I just don't want to be here anymore." She gasped for air. This was no longer Vera the comedienne, poking fun at her weight. This was a shell of a woman, filling the void inside until there was no room left for her heart. She was eating herself to death.

How could I save her?

"What about a nice cup of tea?" I said.

I wasn't sure she'd heard me, but gradually her breathing slowed, and she reached out to stroke the cat curled on the table next to her.

"With cookies?" she said without looking up.

"Of course."

Dipping teabags in hot water was comforting, as was arranging a perfect circle of pinwheel cookies on a glass plate. "Why don't I pull up a chair next to you?" I asked. "We can share the table."

She shooed the cat off the table with a swipe of her arm. We sipped and dunked to the accompaniment of a tinkling piano piece that sounded like a music box.

"Do you know that piece?" she asked.

"Not really, but it sounds a little like a music box I had as a kid." That wasn't true. It sounded like a music box someone had given me at my baby shower. The gift was still in the closet—a clown-covered tin box gathering dust in a lonely yellow room.

"You got kids?" she asked.

"No. Not yet." *Maybe never.*

She dunked the last of the cookies and sucked on its mushy end. "I think some children are born into the wrong families, while the right families have empty spaces where children should be." She held out a tissue. "Your mascara's running. Fix yourself up. Bathroom's down the hall, second door on the left."

My grief passed as quickly as it had come, though I knew that wasn't the end of it. I checked myself in the mirror of a partially open medicine cabinet. An invitation. Inside were aspirin bottles, Band-Aids, mouthwash, nail polish remover, cotton balls, but no prescription drugs—nothing one would expect to see in the medicine cabinet of someone as morbidly obese as Vera: cholesterol meds, blood pressure meds, syringes for insulin. She was, as advertised, healthy as a horse.

When I got back, Vera was looking out the window. She'd opened the curtains and stood motionless, backlit by the late afternoon sun.

"I'd like to get out some time. Sit on a park bench somewhere. It's been a long time. Used to pick stuff up at the grocery store, but now they deliver. Anything I want."

"Are you asking me out?"

She smiled.

The day of our outing, Vera wore those dangly earrings and had outlined her coral lipstick in a darker shade. I'd been right about her mouth—movie-star quality. From the neck up, it looked like she was trying.

It took us a long time to negotiate the staircase from her second-floor apartment to the front door. I followed behind as she slowly made her way down. Halfway, one of her flip-flops slipped off and landed on the step below. I reached out to support her, but she brushed my hand away. Leaning heavily on the railing, she succeeded in snagging the strap with her toes, and then continued her descent.

Finally, we were out the door, down a few marble steps, and into tree-lined Delancey Street, which was dappled with afternoon sunlight. Vera smoothed her dress, which had ridden up in the back. It was a housedress, like my grandmother used to wear. I didn't think they sold stuff like that anymore.

We made our way slowly down the block of stately nineteenth-century homes and around the corner toward a pocket park. But we were waylaid by a luncheonette. Vera paused to stare at a flyer on the wall, and by the time we sat down, her mood had changed from sunny to sullen. I fiddled with the tableware and checked the menu. "You know what you want?" I asked.

"My sister took a master class with that pianist in the poster. He's going to be playing Mozart's Twenty-first Piano Concerto—the one from that old movie. I forget the name. And the orchestra's doing *Carnival of the Animals*."

"I'm afraid I don't know much about classical."

"Well, *Carnival's* fun. First time I heard it was at a children's concert. They showed cartoons that went along with the music. Every kid should be that lucky."

I had no response.

She picked up the menu and then put it down as the waitress approached. "I know what I want," she said before the girl had a chance to pull the pencil out from behind her ear. "Large burger, medium well with extra cheese, large fries, and a black-and-white milkshake." Then she noticed a woman at the next table staring at her and shaking her head. "And whipped cream, honey. Lots of whipped cream," she added in a booming voice that turned heads.

Vera picked at her cuticle with little stabbing motions, her face flushed. Though she'd never admit it, Vera did care about people's reactions. The woman next to us shook her head and tsk-tsked a couple of times before turning to her friend and whispering something. Had I been in that woman's place before I knew Vera, I might have done the same. Instead, I ordered a bacon burger in solidarity, though I'd been meaning to have a salad.

"Would you like to see it again, Vera? *Carnival of the Animals?*"

"Let me think about it," she said, looking over at the grill as the cook plunged a basket of fries in hot oil. "Don't you just hate it when people tell you what to do?" Vera asked loudly.

"What?"

"That sign over there: 'We do not serve alcohol to pregnant women.' What right do they have to decide what we can or can't put into our bodies?"

The waitress brought the milkshake, and Vera took a long pull on the straw before answering my question. "Yes to the concert. Don't pick me up; I'll take a cab. We'll need a box; regular seats are too small. I'll pay. Don't wait for me if I'm late. I'll be there." Her words came out in a rush, as if she were afraid she'd change her mind.

The chime announcing the start of the concert sounded a second time, and Vera still hadn't arrived at the concert hall. Only a few stragglers and latecomers remained in the lobby. Maybe she couldn't find anything that fit, or couldn't make it down the steps, or found the idea of showing herself at a public event too daunting. All week I'd resisted the urge to call her and offer help, reminding myself this wasn't a rescue mission and I wasn't her mother. I'd called that morning, and she'd assured me we were still on.

The usher showed me to my seat, and they shut the doors. Damn. I picked up the program and tried to follow the play-by-play. *The music begins with a march figure and quickly moves to a more lyrical melody.* She might be out in the lobby, watching on the monitor. *The soloist plays a brief cadenza before resolving to a trill on the dominant G.* I bet she knows all this stuff. Probably heard her sister practice it a hundred times. *The famous andante is in three parts starting with an orchestra introduction to the solo piano in F major.* She could be lying in a pool of blood or choking on a chicken bone.

Finally, the music was over. Out in the lobby, I called Vera. No answer. The chime signaled the end of the intermission. Another call. Still no answer. The ushers closed the doors, and I heard applause coming from the monitor as the conductor mounted the podium. I stepped outside and hailed a cab.

In the vestibule of her building, I buzzed her apartment. No answer. Buzzed again. Nothing. I was about to ring another apartment when a man opened the door and stepped out.

"Vera," I said, as I slipped past him. "She's my friend."

I took the stairs two at a time.

Her door was unlocked, and I went in, calling her name softly, then louder. Silence. No movement in the living room. I headed down the hall. No one in the kitchen, and an empty Sara Lee box on the counter. She wouldn't have stuffed her face if she planned to do away with herself, would she? Unless she had planned for her gateway pastry to be her last meal. "Vera!" Bedroom empty. "Vera!" Bathroom door closed. My hand shook as I turned the knob. Bathtub blessedly empty. Then I heard it—an oooo sound coming from the living room, starting low and rising like an approaching siren. Keening.

Vera was sitting on the floor, her back against the front of the loveseat. The back of the chair had hidden her from view. She clutched a framed picture to her chest, much the same way she cradled the cookie box the first time we met. She didn't look up when I called her name—just rocked and made that sound. I sat down next to her and reached an arm around her shoulder. She took a couple of deep breaths and rested the photo on her thighs. It was the blond boy at Love Park.

"His name was Robbie, and he was ten when this picture was taken," she said in a voice potholed with grief. "I visited him at his foster home a few times. Knew from the first visit I was going to adopt him. The family curse be damned." The words came slowly. "I got the feeling the foster...parents were in it for the money, and in the market for a younger kid. To restart the funds. That's what some of those scumbags do."

She stopped, and I rubbed her shoulder.

"I did the adoption paperwork. Robbie and I went on a bunch of outings together. Trying each other out. I took him to the children's concert—*Carnival of the Animals*—and he loved it." She chuckled and then sobbed. "Two days before the adoption date, I took him to the park." She looked down at the picture. "He'd saved money to buy me an ice cream cone. It had to be peppermint, he told me, since that was his favorite. I told him that was my favorite too and bought one for him. I can still taste the...pinkness. I told him this is what happiness tastes like." Her voice dropped. "The foster parents, those bastards, beat him where it didn't show...probably been doing it for years." She spat out the *p*s and *d*s, slashing the air with her words. "I saw him with the foster parents so many times. He never said anything. Never acted scared when he was with them. But I should have known anyway. Known they'd go too far. It was my job to save him. I couldn't save my family, and he'd become all the family I needed."

She went on so quietly I could barely hear. "That last time, they hit him so hard something ruptured inside. By the time they got him to the hospital, he was gone. I should have known." She sobbed, tears pooling in the folds of her skin.

"How could you know? Kids are good at hiding things."

She went on as if she hadn't heard me. "I should have figured out what they were doing. It was my *job*, what I'd been trained to do—get them out of danger, save those babies." Long pause. "Today would have been his birthday. His twelfth."

And in a what-if world of no miscarriages, my first child would have been two years old.

I got on my knees and twisted my body so I could put my arms around her as far as they would go. "Maybe you didn't save him, but for the two years you knew him, he was a part of your life and you were a part of his. You made him happy."

Vera's flesh was soft, comforting as a down pillow. I buried my head in her chest and she rested her head on my shoulder. We sat there a long time, hugging each other like mother and child.

One Last Thing

"It's time, Nora. Get the powder I ordered, mix it in the liquid, and feed it to me. They say the end will be quick and painless."

"No, Jeffrey." Hands on hips, she looked down at him in his motorized wheelchair. "I won't do it. You promised we'd try that one last thing before you…"

"Self-terminate."

"Not funny. You promised to try it," she said, casting a quick glance back at the door to the living room. "He's waiting for us in the other room. I'll let him in." She turned and took a step toward the door.

"Don't."

"Why not?"

"I changed my mind. It's not going to work."

"Jeffrey." She turned back and knelt in front of him so they were eye to eye. "Love. How can I get you to—"

"Change my mind back. Question mark."

"You don't have to do that punctuation thing, Jeffrey. I know when you're asking a question."

"And I know you're going to tell me I have so much to live for."

"You have so much to live for."

"Why would anyone who looks like this want to go on living. Question mark."

She exhaled a puff of air. "But you're not just anyone, Jeffrey. Remember what the *Times* said about your debut novel*?*"

"Fuck the *Times*."

"Groundbreaking. A work of genius. Yours is a voice that needs to be heard."

"My voice. Now that's a hoot. I'd laugh if I could, but there's a fucking hole in my throat where my voice used to be."

"You know what I mean," she said softly, resting her hands on his bony shoulders.

"And *you* know what *I* mean." He touched a button on his armrest, jerking his chair backward, tired of having the same damn argument over and over.

"*I* hear your voice, Jeffrey."

"Don't talk to me in metaphors. What you hear is the fucking squawk that comes out of this synthesizer."

"It *is* your real voice. They used your voice as the prototype."

"Don't patronize me. I can hear what it sounds like. An android. A lobotomized Ken doll. No ups, no downs. Flat, flat, flat." He lurched his chair backward and forward and back again, visually punctuating his frustration.

Unbalanced by the sudden movement, Nora barely managed to stay on her feet. "That's not true. You can still move your eyes, your hands. Stephen Hawking couldn't move…"

"Stephen fucking Hawking. Insert scream-face emoji here."

Nora rolled her eyes; then she blushed at her juvenile reaction. "Hawking was handicapped for fifty years before he died, and it didn't stop him. Discovered black holes, quantum whatever. And all he could move was a muscle in his cheek."

"And that's supposed to inspire me? Hawking was a fucking genius."

"You are, too, Jeffrey. That's what I'm trying to tell you.

That's what they said in the *Times*." She took the framed review off the wall and read, 'His is a voice that will not be silenced. We're eagerly awaiting his next novel.'"

"Ha, ha, ha."

She tapped the glass with her fingernail in time to the words: "*The New York Times*! Your dream. That's what you told me the night we met. You wanted to write a five-star novel that was good enough to be reviewed in the *Times*."

"Well, they reviewed it. So, dream come true, show over, roll the credits."

"This isn't a show, dammit." She slammed the framed review down on a nearby table. "It's our lives together, our love, your dream. When your novel was published, you said it was just the beginning, and your dream wouldn't be complete until you'd written a second one even better than the first. You swore there was no way in hell you'd leave this earth as a one-hit wonder."

"It worked for Sylvia Plath."

"Why do you always do that when I'm being serious. You can't give up now. You've almost finished your second novel."

"You know it's not a novel; it's an autobiography. A sad, pathetic story." Why couldn't she understand that the joy had gone out of writing, that he'd lost the ability to live through his characters now that his only subject was his sorry-assed self.

"Not pathetic. It's *your* story, and it needs to be told. Your editor calls it a masterpiece. Says the world will be moved to tears."

"The world can take a flying leap."

"Damn you." She balled her hands into fists and squeezed her eyes shut. "What about me, Jeffrey?" When she opened her eyes, they were moist. "Look, I'm crying. Your words moved me to tears. Should I take a flying leap?"

"Not funny, as you've told me so many times."

"You're right, but you've got to finish what you started."

"Why? We both know how it ends."

"No, we don't—"

"It ends with a dose of secobarbital."

She shook her head slowly as silence hung heavy as death in the room. "It doesn't have to be that way," she said in a half-whisper.

"Yes it does, dot dot dot."

"What?"

"Ellipsis. It means something's missing."

"I *know* what an ellipsis is. What's missing?"

"You of all people should know the answer to that."

"Me?"

"Yes. It's something you're missing, too. It's something Stephen Hawking never lost. He had three children."

"What's this? A stupid riddle? We're talking life and death here."

"Humor me. Here's another clue. He had three children."

"What?"

"Dr. Black Hole could still get it up. Lost everything but his mind and his manhood."

"You haven't lost yours, either—manhood, I mean. That's why we're trying this one last thing." But even as she said the words, she flashed back to their passionate lovemaking that had slowly faded as his illness progressed. Who was she kidding? She *did* miss it. The heat of pent-up desire coursed through her veins. Her cheeks burned. "The doctor says you're perfectly capable of sexual arousal, since ALS doesn't affect that... reflex."

"What does he know? He's not trapped in this frozen shell of a body."

"He says you're depressed. There are things we could... that's why we're trying this one last thing."

"Nora, would you please give it a rest. Just stop talking. Exclamation point. Exclamation point."

"Jeffrey, love, you're crying."

"I'm not..."

"Oh baby. Let me." She took a tissue from the box on the table and wiped his eyes. "There, that's better."

"If I could just…just make love to you once more. If I could feel that passion, for even a moment, I'd remember what it's like to be alive. Look at me, Nora. I'm already a dead man."

"No you're not, love." She wanted to believe that. She fantasized about the two of them when she was alone in bed at night. "We can try to bring that part of you back to life."

"No point. The pill didn't work. And you tried everything. You touched, stroked, acted the slut, talked dirty, wore leather, wore nothing. You debased yourself for me."

"Debased? That was me loving you." She pressed her hand to her heart, then to his chest.

"You loving me, and I couldn't love you back."

"So it's time to try that one last thing. You said the thought of watching me make love to someone else like I made love to you, stirred something inside you."

"I changed my mind. My body's broken, Nora. I'm empty."

"'The image of you making love stirred something inside me.' Those were your exact words." Even as she spoke, a wave of anticipation washed over her as she thought of the man waiting outside the room.

"Mmm."

"You said it turned you on."

"I said, 'Stirred something inside.' Not the same."

"But it could be. Remember when we fantasized about doing something like this?"

"Yeah, in my other life."

"It's still your life. I love you, Jeffrey. I'm doing this for both of us." But she was no longer sure that was true, as she was now finding it hard to ignore thoughts of her own pleasure.

"You're not going to let this idea we had go, are you?"

"No, we're in this together."

"*Not* together. *I'm* the one who's suffering. Why can't you just…I'm so tired, Nora. I can't argue anymore."

"So, I should call him in?"

"Yes, dammit. Let's get this over with."

"Daniel, would you come in please," she said, her voice

soft and tentative. She cleared her throat and summoned him again, this time with more authority. The door opened.

"Oh my God."

"What is it, Jeffrey?"

"He looks so much like me. Like I used to..." This was hell. What had he been thinking when he agreed to this?

"I want you to feel what he's feeling. Where do you want us to do it?"

"Couch, floor, against the wall, doesn't matter."

"You loved it on the floor."

"Nora, you don't have to do this." He wanted to reach out and grab her, cover her with his useless body.

"Yes, I do. I've told him how we like to do it."

"*Liked* to do it." That man was already taking his place. Even if he closed his eyes, it wouldn't block out the sounds, the memories.

"Imagine you're him, Jeffrey." She nodded to Daniel, and he undressed. His body looked so much like her husband's before he'd gotten sick. Muscular, unblemished. She had called Jeffrey her Adonis. In her fantasies she'd never been unfaithful to Jeffrey, so the resemblance was oddly comforting. Next, at her prompting, Daniel began to take off her clothes. "See. He's undressing me just the way you did."

"I'm missing...dot dot dot. Dot dot dot." How could he stop her? Even if he had his real voice, there were not enough words in the English language to describe what he was feeling. "Your body. So beautiful, Nora. If I could only touch you."

"You can. I'm doing this with you, love."

"Nora!"

"And this...and this...and—"

"Nora. Please stop. I can't take it. Exclamation point. Exclamation. Exclama—"

"Oh, Jeffrey." She had no idea how much she'd missed the touching, the loving, the joy of being alive.

"Over here, Nora. *I'm* Jeffrey. I'm *still* Jeffrey. Please..."

"Please. Don't. Stop. Yes."

No, he screamed silently at his powerlessness to stop what was happening "Missing. Missing."

"Yes. Yes. Y*es*!"

"Nora. Please look at me, Nora. I have something to tell you. Why aren't you listening to me?"

"Oh God, it's been so long." She lay next to Daniel, the carpet tickling her naked back. She reached over and kneaded his chest, and he moved closer.

"Nora. Listen to me. I've changed my mind. I can't watch any more. I'm closing my eyes. Nora. I'm begging you to stop. Exclamation point. How long have you and this man..."

"Daniel. His name is Daniel, and this is the first time we've done..."

"We can try again, Nora," said Jeffrey.

She got up slowly, reluctantly, still awash in guilt-tinged ecstasy. "Did you feel anything when you watched?" she asked as she put on her underwear.

"I felt...sad. But we can try again. Next time I swear I'll... why are you looking at me like that?"

She was being pulled apart by memories of the past, realities of the life she was living, possibilities of the life that awaited her. The struggle left her speechless.

"Say something. Please."

She shook her head. "I...I don't know, Jeffrey."

"Don't look at me like that. Like you don't see me."

"I think we were fooling ourselves to think this would work."

"Send that man away. Then let me prove that I can be a man."

"Daniel, would you please get dressed and go home." God help her, she wanted him to stay there on the floor, naked and magnificent. But she said nothing as he dressed and left the room. Then she turned back to Jeffrey, tearful and silent.

I hear your question, he thought. How are you going to prove that you can still be a man? "I can still move these." He wiggled his fingers. "Take my hand, let me touch you."

Her eyes did not leave his as she lifted his hand and pressed it to her breast. She felt his fingers tapping feebly against her skin. Tears flowing, she waited as the room drowned in silence. His eyes were brown pools of despair. She gently placed his hand back in his lap, an act of inexpressible sadness and finality.

"I was right when I said it was time for me to go. I have no words left to write. And I'll never be able to touch you the way he can, so it will be nothing but frustration for both of us."

Her tears were salty on her tongue. "What do you want me to do, Jeffrey?"

"One last thing. Get the powder, mix it in the liquid, and feed it to me. They say the end will be quick and painless, and then both of us can move on."

Mean Girl

The Cresheim Court Senior Living library was usually unoccupied before lunch, so the presence of someone inside the dark-paneled room caught Annette's eye. She didn't recognize the woman—probably a new arrival—so she opened the glass doors and stepped inside the room to introduce herself to the newcomer.

"Welcome to Cresheim," she said, extending her hand. "I'm Annette Lavazza, and you are…"

"Margaret McGinley," the woman said in a soft voice, reaching out her hand. "Pleased to meet you."

Her parchment skin felt so fragile that Annette was afraid to squeeze too hard. Margaret was sitting in a leather tufted chair by a window, and the light was not kind to her. She was one of the *old* old, well north of ninety, at least ten years older than Annette and her friends. She won't be sitting at our table, Annette thought as she plunked herself down on a tufted wingback chair across from Margaret. "I assumed you were new, since I know just about everyone here. When did you move in?"

"Yesterday."

"Guess you're still a little discombobulated from the move."

"Oh, my son and daughter were such a big help, they made it easy for me."

"I'll bet," said Annette. "They're always trying to get us out of our homes and into senior housing, aren't they? I told my Joanie I was perfectly capable of living on my own, but—"

"Oh, no." Her smile revealed a set of large teeth and a pronounced overbite. "My children wanted me to stay put. Thought I'd be happier in my own home. *I* was the one who told them it was time."

"Well, aren't you the lucky one," said Annette, instantly regretting the note of sarcasm that had slipped through. She put on her brightest smile before launching into her standard spiel about the ins and outs of Cresheim Court. She tried not to stare at Margaret's gray, cotton-candy hair, which barely covered her head, and the patches of pink scalp the color of mouse ears. Annette smoothed her red-highlighted chestnut coiffure in a subconscious gesture of reassurance. Margaret nodded as Annette spoke, but didn't have much to add, and Annette pegged her as an introvert. Too bad. Extroverts like herself had it so much easier.

Annette noticed a leather-bound journal open on Margaret's lap, with a silver pen cradled in the fold. "I'm sorry. I won't bother you any longer," she said.

"No bother," she said. But her arthritic fingers were already grasping the pen.

"What are you writing?" asked Annette in an effort to be polite.

"My memoirs. The children asked me to record my stories for the grandkids."

Annette left her with a promise to be in touch and walked away with a vague feeling of uneasiness.

That evening, Margaret walked up to the table where Annette was having dinner with her friends Darlene and Christine. She hooked her fingers over the back of the empty chair and asked, "May I join you ladies?" The two friends looked at Annette, who pointed her fork at the empty chair next to her. "Sorry," she said, trying to sound sorry. "This seat is taken."

Annette watched Margaret look around the table at the half-eaten meals. Dinner had long been underway, and it was obvious no one would be taking that seat. Margaret's fingers tightened on the chair back; then she sighed and shuffled off, leaning heavily on her cane. Annette watched as she made her way to a half-empty table at the far end of the dining hall and lowered herself into a chair.

"Someone that old should be in assisted living, don't you think?" said Christine, her penciled brows rising above heavily mascaraed eyelashes. Seventy-eight and dumpling-shaped, Christine was the youngest at the table. Like Annette, she was from South Philly.

"You got that right, Chrissie." She watched her friend tuck into her chicken breast and wondered how anyone could take such pleasure in dry, overcooked poultry; all the corn-starched gravy in the world couldn't hide the damage they'd done in the kitchen. Christine was a chowhound, as evidenced by the food-stained napkin tucked under her chin. Annette would attempt a few more bites, but most of the meals nowadays tasted more like cardboard than food. Must be a new cook, she thought, though her friends seemed to be having no problem with their dinners. Christine's mound of mashed potatoes was now a pockmarked lunar landscape, and Darlene had hoovered up everything on her plate. It would be so easy to fix the food, Annette thought. More butter in the potatoes and less thickener in the gravy would have gone a long way. Annette used to make a hell of a Thanksgiving dinner back in the day. Nowadays she wouldn't even attempt to cook in the pint-sized kitchen that came with her apartment. Not that she missed it, she told herself.

"S'matter, Annette?" Darlene asked before digging into her chocolate pudding. "Sad about Bea?" Tall, skinny Darlene could pack away food like nobody's business and never gain an ounce. Though being thin in old age often translated into a gaunt face and questions about the state of one's health, her fiery red bouffant drew attention away from facial imperfections.

Annette glanced at the place setting where Bea used to sit. Before Bea had moved in, Annette and her friends had called themselves the Three Mouseketeers, after three of the original Mickey Mouse Club members from the old TV show, whose names they shared. When Bea came along, they'd rechristened themselves the Four Mouseketeers. "There wasn't anyone named Bea on the show," Annette told her, "but I'm going to make you an honorary member because I like you." The other ladies accepted her because Annette did. And now Bea was gone. The day before she died, she and Annette had walked in the mall, as they did every Tuesday before having their hair and nails done. The following morning, a nursing aide found Bea slumped on the floor next to her bed. Cerebral hemorrhage, the doctor said. Gone just like that. At the funeral, Annette imagined Bea looking down at herself and thanking God she'd gotten that last appointment at the salon. That's what she'd loved about Bea.

Annette pushed the string beans around on her plate before putting down her fork. "Course I'm sad about Bea. But the reason I'm not eating is on account of the food is crap."

"Crap?" Darlene looked down at her empty plate.

"Yeah, crap. Let me spell it out for you in plain English. S-H-I-T." Her friends howled, and Annette joined in. *I've still got it,* she thought.

"I miss her," Christine said, wiping pudding off her mouth.

"Yeah." Annette raised her coffee cup. "To Bea. God bless her, wherever she is."

Darlene tried to do the same, but her hand shook, sloshing coffee over the sides of the cup. "Damn tremor," she muttered as she slowly lowered the cup to her saucer with both hands. "To Bea," she said, lowering her head to take a sip.

After dessert, Christine and Darlene got up and walked out to the lobby, but Annette lingered, checking her image in the mirror along the far wall. From that distance she looked pretty good. Her hair was the same chestnut color it was when she was a cheerleader, thanks to Monsieur Henri, though it was much shorter now—her concession to age-appropriate hair-styles. She straightened her back—no dowager's hump, thank God—proud of her slim figure. She'd always had that going for her. And an ample bosom to top it off.

As she made her way slowly up the center aisle between the tables to the lobby, she stopped to schmooze. Life imitating middle school, she thought, people seeking their own. She had a nickname for each table: the popular girls like herself, the Mahjongs, the Canastas, the knitters. Even a table of single men. Over the years a few of them had paired off with female residents, leaving their respective tables, and some of the couples even lived together. Who knew what they did when they were alone.

Margaret was sitting at the last table by the door with a couple of the intellectuals—Annette's name for the ladies who went downtown to concerts, plays, and lectures, even though the center had perfectly good entertainment right there. Margaret's companions were talking, but not to her. Margaret didn't seem to mind. Her features were relaxed, as if she were meditating. Guess I should be polite, Annette thought.

"Looks like you're getting into the swing of things, Margaret. I'll catch you later."

Margaret nodded, and Annette continued on, past the scrum of walkers parked outside the dining room and into the lobby. Residents could eat in the independent living dining room as long as they didn't need wheelchairs or walkers to get to their tables. She was headed toward her friends, who were waiting for her outside the dining room, when Evelyn, the receptionist, called to her from the front desk. When Annette looked over, Evelyn made a beckoning gesture.

"'Scuse me, girls," said Annette. "Back in a sec."

By the time Annette got to the desk, Evelyn was on the phone, but she held up a finger for Annette to wait.

"You must be so proud of your daughter," she said when she hung up.

Proud of what? Annette tried to match Evelyn's smile. "Yes, I—"

"Such a nice article in the paper. Front page of the features section." She held up a folded copy of the *Inquirer*. Under the headline "Consultant to the Rich and Famous" was a picture of Annette's daughter with the CEO of a major cable company.

"Oh. That." Annette smiled as if she'd already known her daughter was featured in the paper. Had Joan told her about it? Maybe, but her daughter was out of town on business trips so much of the time...

Three years earlier, when Annette was still living in her own home, she'd tried to convince her daughter that she wasn't too old to live alone, but Joan told her she was deluding herself. "Who's going to take care of you if you get really sick?" Joan asked. "What happens if you fall?"

"I wear that thingy around my neck that calls nine-one-one. And I do Silver Sneakers, Zumba, and line dancing," she had told Joan. "Got all my original parts: teeth, knees, hips, even ovaries, though they don't do me much good anymore." She looked at her daughter, hoping for a smile, but Joan shook her head and telephoned the next senior residence on her list. Annette should have known better than to expect Joan to laugh at her jokes. At least everyone else did.

"Here." Evelyn handed Annette the paper. "In case your copy got messed up."

"Thanks, hon," Annette said. She refrained from looking at the article and slipped it into her tote bag, keeping up the fiction that she'd already read it. She'd look at it later, after she met up with her friends.

"We better hustle if we wanna make the movie," Christine said.

The Robert Redford film was something she'd been looking forward to, but the newspaper in her tote bag had taken priority. "Sorry, girls, I changed my mind. I'm feeling kind of tired, so I think I'll go upstairs, get into my nightie, and maybe watch that comedy special on HBO."

"You don't look so good, Nettie. Hope you're not coming down with something," said Darlene.

"Me? Never."

Annette took a peek at the features section as she rode up on the elevator. There, spanning three columns, was the photo of her daughter, all chestnut hair and white teeth. Joan was wearing a tailored suit jacket with padded shoulders. Her scoop-necked top revealed just enough cleavage to catch the reader's eye. No one would guess her daughter was almost sixty. Annette had looked like that at Joan's age, too, and she had the pictures to prove it.

When the elevator bumped to a stop, she stuffed the newspaper into her bag and stepped into the corridor. The busy black-on-gray pattern of the carpet made her dizzy when she walked down the hall. How had she missed the disorienting effect of the floor covering until now? *Are they trying to drive us crazy? It's a wonder someone hasn't walked into a wall. I'll have to talk to someone about that. Somebody has to speak up.* She straightened the Christmas wreath on her door, a swirl of shiny gift boxes, curled paper, and greenery. The nicest wreath on the floor, she thought, like her apartment. At least Joan had given her that.

Annette stretched out on her chaise lounge in the den and read the article, which went on for two pages about her high-powered consultant daughter and the famous executives she coached. On the second page were pictures of Joan with the CEO of Merrill Lynch, a senior vice president of Blue Cross, and the Dalai Lama. Yes, her daughter could afford to pay for her two-bedroom, two-bath at Cresheim; it was the least she could do. Annette ran a finger under each line of print as she reread the article. Not a word about how she and Tony had struggled to send their daughter to an Ivy League school on a cop's salary and the little Annette made as a school secretary. Nothing about the smarts that Joan had inherited from Tony, who'd graduated second in his class at South Philly High. His classmates tended to forget how smart he was, remembering him only as captain of the football team, class heartthrob, and steady boyfriend of the girl voted most popular in the class.

Annette looked at the photograph on the bookshelf of herself at sixteen, waving pompoms in her skimpy cheerleader skirt. Now she and Christine were the only ones left who remembered how it had been in high school. She wondered if Margaret had read the *Inquirer* article and perhaps realized Joan was Annette's daughter. Joan had kept her maiden name—Lavazza wasn't a name you heard every day—and people always told her there was a family resemblance. Annette spread the article out on the coffee table so none of her visitors would miss it.

For the next two weeks, whenever there was a pause in the dinner conversation, Annette would look over at the far table by the door. Sometimes Margaret sat with a couple of other women, and sometimes she sat alone, reading a book. One night she was writing in her journal. Her memoir, she'd said. One of the volunteers offered a memoir-writing class in the library, so other residents besides Margaret must have been working on memoirs as well, but not anyone she knew. What do you even put in a memoir if you'd lived in Philly your whole life, were voted most popular in high school, married a local guy, had two children, baked cookies, etcetera? Her son and daughter knew everything about her, so what was the point of writing about it? And the grandkids had moved to California and rarely came east. They probably weren't interested.

What was so memoir-worthy about Margaret, a woman who kept to herself and didn't seem to have any friends? Reminded her of the smart kids in high school who thought they were so much better than the rest. Not that they'd ever admitted it, but Annette could tell from their expressions when they'd looked at her, something about the downward tilt of their mouths, as if they'd just eaten something sour.

She couldn't stop wondering what made Margaret's life so interesting that it was worth writing about, even at the dinner table. The question was always there at the back of her mind, like an itch she couldn't scratch. So, that night, she told her friends she wouldn't be joining them for dinner the following evening because she was expecting a call from her daughter. Not exactly a lie. It was possible, though unlikely, that her daughter would call.

The next morning, she stopped at the front desk and asked for Margaret's room number, explaining that she had something to give her. That night Margaret heated up a frozen pizza and watched the five o'clock news. When she was sure everyone would be at dinner, she walked down the hall to apartment 721 and leaned in to read the little gold name tag on the door: Margaret McGinley. An old maid's name. Many residents didn't keep valuables around and left their doors unlocked unless they were going to spend time out of the building. Maybe Margaret was one of them. Annette tentatively turned the knob and gave the door a little push with her hip. It opened.

She took a deep breath and hesitated briefly before slipping inside and closing the door behind her. A single hurricane lamp cast a dim light into a living room obscured by heavy damask curtains and weighted down with dark wood furniture, bookshelves, and knickknacks. There was a hint of cabbage in the air. Cabbage: the poster-child odor of old age. Didn't Margaret know enough to use a room freshener? And was that a toaster oven on the counter of the tiny kitchen? A potential fire hazard for someone whose memory might be slipping, someone who might forget to turn it off.

Annette stood by the closed door, an intruder, momentarily paralyzed by two conflicting emotions: discomfort at being an intruder and excitement about what she might discover. Excitement won out. She proceeded into the living room, her footsteps muffled by a plush oriental carpet. She picked up a small purse from the narrow table near the door and riffled through it. She wasn't looking for anything specific but was somehow disappointed to find nothing more than health insurance cards, an AARP card, and a few dollar bills.

Annette checked her watch. The dining room had just opened and dinner was about to be served, so she had plenty of time. She turned on another lamp to get a better look at the pictures on the wall and the framed photographs on the tables. There were photos of Margaret as a bride in a simple white dress that complemented her slightly overweight but shapely figure. She was looking up at the bridegroom with a subtle, Mona Lisa kind of smile, and he met her gaze with a slight, satisfied smile on his own lips. There were photos of the couple with two children, a boy and a girl, graduation photos of their son and daughter, and pictures with grandchildren. There was a photo of a large group of people standing in a field, wearing identical T-shirts. She leaned in to read the printing: McGinley Family Reunion.

Annette went into the bedroom and turned on the light. On the wall next to the bed was a photograph of Margaret, young and smiling, accepting an award. She'd put on a little weight since her wedding. Annette moved closer and read the plaque at the bottom of the frame, which identified her as Margaret McGinley Cowan, Teacher of the Year. The resemblance to Eleanor Roosevelt was unmistakable: the same oversized, protruding teeth and shapeless figure. Margaret had never been an attractive woman, not even at an age when youth bestowed a veneer of beauty on the plainest of features. Next to the photo was a framed diploma from Temple University awarding the degree of Doctor of Philosophy in Media and Communications to Margaret M. Cowan. So she was a Ph.D.

Tony had talked about getting a Ph.D. in science or math when the two of them were in their first year at Temple. But there wasn't enough money for tuition after Joan was born and then Christopher, so first Annette and then Tony had dropped out of college. Annette hadn't been much of a student, but Tony would definitely have gotten his Ph.D. if he'd had the opportunity. He was that smart. Joanie had inherited his smarts, as had Chris, though her son squandered them moving from one dead-end job to another, doing God knows what, out in California.

Annette walked over to an antique dresser and opened a drawer. She'd forgotten she was still clutching Margaret's purse and set it down on top of the dresser. Then she reached into the drawer and pulled a nightgown out from a neatly folded pile. Running her thumb over the fabric, she closed her eyes, as if the off-white lace and faded pink silk could reveal the essence of its wearer. She refolded the nightgown, put it back in the drawer, and was about to close it when she remembered the purse. In an impulsive move, she stuffed the purse behind a stack of underwear and closed the drawer. The act was reminiscent of the practical jokes she used to play on her friends. But Margaret wasn't a friend. Would she think a poltergeist had paid a visit to her apartment, or perhaps think it had been her own doing? Annette hesitated briefly at the bedroom door before turning off the light and walking through the living room and out into the hall.

Darlene called her a couple days later. "Margaret thinks she may be losing it," she said.

Annette exhaled softly, as if to expel the irrational fear that Darlene knew what she'd done in Margaret's room. She waited for her friend to continue.

"Yesterday was Dr. Richmond's visiting day. I had an appointment and was in the waiting room when Margaret came out with the doctor. They were talking softly, but you know how good my hearing is. Anyway, I'm pretty sure she said, 'Well, I hope it's just forgetfulness and not something more.' And he said, 'Why don't I schedule a few tests?'"

A feather of guilt tickled Annette's conscience and then floated off.

There was usually a card game going on in the social room, and Annette was up for some company, especially since today was her birthday. But when she peered in through the glass door, the room appeared to be empty. Since she couldn't see the far corners, she walked in to take a closer look. The social room, like the library, had a distinctly masculine feel, with its dark wood paneling and maroon carpeting. It was a surprising choice of décor for a predominantly female population. The same decorator must have done both rooms. In the library, the Christmas decorations and the fire blazing in the fireplace warmed the room nicely.

There were no card players there, but a lone figure hunched over a card table. Squinting, Annette recognized Gordon Lindhurst, a retired physician and one of the few men at Ravenwood. Tall, with a fine head of white hair, he always had a kind word for the ladies. More than one of her acquaintances had called him a good catch, though he must have been close to ninety. She'd exchanged a few words with him in the past, but she'd never had the opportunity to engage him. Her birthday might be her lucky day.

He didn't hear her approach, and she was able to get close enough to see that he was working on a jigsaw puzzle. She watched the movement of his long fingers as they closed around the puzzle pieces and the confidence with which he snapped them into place. He looked up and smiled at her, which she took as an invitation to move closer. "May I join you?"

"Sure. Two sets of eyes are always better than one." His voice was low and resonant, and his eyes were welcoming. He must have had a great bedside manner.

She sat down next to him and picked up the puzzle box. On its front was a picture of an island beach in shades of blue, green, turquoise, and white. Not an easy puzzle, with all that water.

"Where are your friends?" he asked.

"Longwood Gardens, all dolled up for Christmas. They asked me to go with them, but to be honest, I was never a big fan of flowers."

"My wife used to drag me there and to the flower show, but I hated the crowds."

"Me, too. And when I looked at those mountains of flowers, all I could think of was hay fever."

He laughed, and she felt younger. Picking up an edge piece, she handed it to him, and their fingers touched. *Perhaps...*

"Thanks." He fitted the piece in place. "I hear it's your birthday."

"How—"

"Word gets around. You're a popular lady. Happy birthday."

"Oh, I wouldn't say that. But I'm flattered," she said, blushing and lowering her eyes. She picked up one of the undifferentiated blue puzzle pieces. Her hand hovered a moment over the mass of blue; then she miraculously placed the piece exactly where it belonged.

She looked up at him, saw his eyebrows raised in surprise, and smiled. "Lucky guess."

They worked in comfortable silence, like two people who had been together a long time. She'd forgotten how it felt to be in a relationship where all the pieces fit.

"May I join you?" came a woman's voice.

Annette's fingers tightened around a puzzle piece. *Say no.*

Gordon raised his head. "Of course, Margaret." He gave her the same inviting smile he'd given Annette. (Or was it warmer? How can you measure a smile?)

Margaret sat down next to Annette, and the two women nodded to each other. Annette's face burned, as if she'd been caught in the act of spying. Margaret opened her mouth to speak, but before she could get a word out, Annette looked at her watch. "Oh, I forgot. I'm expecting a call from my daughter." She stood up.

"Sorry you have to go so soon," said Gordon.

Did he mean that? She was about to respond when she heard him say, "Why don't you move around next to me, Margaret." Annette hurried across the room, surprised by the tears that stung her eyes. She stopped just inside the door of the library to compose herself, and in no time, she was her old self, at least on the outside. She chatted with the people she ran into on her way to her apartment and made them smile.

Annette spent the afternoon in her apartment, trying to distract herself with television. The more she replayed her recent encounter with Gordon, the better she felt. His smile, his laugh. He *had* enjoyed her company. And he was a gentleman, so of course he'd welcomed Margaret, too. Annette put on her new green pants suit and matching shoes with little heels.

On her way to dinner that night, she saw Gordon up ahead, his white head towering over a sea of gray. She rushed to catch up but stopped when she saw Margaret walking beside him. Margaret wasn't using her cane, and Gordon had his arm around her waist. Annette saw him lean in to tell her something; she watched as Margaret tilted up her face and smiled at him. Like in that wedding picture. Annette was close enough to hear him say, "Don't worry, Maggie." *Maggie*. Annette could almost feel Tony's hand on her back, almost hear the loving words he used to whisper in her ear—before he walked out on her. His leaving had been a surprise—even more so because the other woman had been older than Annette.

Annette was waylaid by people wishing her a happy birthday, telling her how good she looked; by the time she made it into the dining room, Margaret and Gordon had seated themselves at a table near the door. She felt her good will withering like week-old flowers, and she wanted to hurry past, but Gordon waved and smiled. *An invitation to join them?* She walked over to their table and made small talk. They wished her a happy birthday. She got them laughing with a sarcastic comment about the meals at Cresheim Court. She waited, hoping. But the two of them resumed their conversation, and she made her way to the "popular girls" table, where her friends hugged her and complimented her on her new outfit. This was where she belonged.

At dinner, she tried to concentrate on the birthday wishes she received from staff and residents. More than one person told her they couldn't believe she was eighty. Gordon was right. She was a popular lady.

After dinner, someone dimmed the lights, and one of the wait staff carried in a cake, candles ablaze. She set it down on a small table at the front of the room and called the "birthday girl" up to blow out the candles. Annette smiled when she saw that the cake was Mickey Mouse-shaped (how had they attached those ears?). She felt special—the other residents had to make do with the standard icing swirls and fleurettes, but not her. As people began singing happy birthday, Annette looked over at the far table, where Margaret and Gordon were talking, not singing, and she felt a heaviness in her chest. When had the rules changed? For most of her life she'd had no trouble snagging men, but now she had no idea what they wanted.

She looked over at Christine, the only one left who remembered her from her high school glory days. Someone called out, "Make a wish." What to wish for? She closed her eyes. For the briefest of moments, she wished she could start life over again. Then she blew out the candles.

Dardanelles

The bracelet fit snugly in her jacket pocket, but the matching necklace she piled on top of it snagged the lining, its pendant leaving an accusing eye dangling over the edge. Marty's other pocket already held a tangle of chains and beads. But this wasn't enough jewelry. She needed something with bigger pockets, something that held more. Scooping out handfuls of jewelry from the pockets, she dumped everything on the floor. Then she started riffling through the other outfits on the rack.

Marty watched from the window of the cruise ship's dining room as darkness covered the last gilded minaret on the shore of a Turkish seaside town. She knew the night's embrace would not be so gentle. A ship churned past, and in its wake came memories of the night Lana had yelled, *You killed him!*

The maître d' gave her grief for reserving a table for one. "Why don't you join that party of Americans?" he suggested. But she held her ground, and tonight she sat at her own table in a dining room that echoed with the clink of silver on china. She picked up her wineglass and took a sip of Cabernet. Then she turned back to the window and caught the reflection of a man and boy at the next table. The man's thick gray hair reminded her of Cole's.

Tonight, the ship would sail through the Dardanelles Strait from Istanbul to the Greek islands, the same route she'd taken with Cole on their honeymoon twenty years ago. They'd stood on deck as the ship cruised the narrow channel separating Europe and Asia, watching the lights playing peek-a-boo along the shore. As the channel widened, the lights grew fainter and seemed to disappear. But then she'd catch a flicker in the distance, like a faint star that can only be seen out the corner of your eye when you're staring at something else.

Cole was an English professor. "With a name like Coleridge, I couldn't sell used cars," he told people when introducing himself. He loved teaching. She once sat in on a class as he read a poem by Yeats with the cadence of an actor. The girls worshipped him, and Marty had wondered what it felt like to be a god, albeit a god who worked at it. Early in their marriage, she caught him pulling jacket after shabby chic tweed jacket out of his closet to see which one worked best with a new pair of jeans. After choosing one, he picked up a hairbrush, put it down, and then spent a moment fluffing out his hair with his fingers.

"Mirror, mirror on the wall," Marty said, standing at the bedroom door. He blushed, and she walked over and hugged him. "Nothing wrong with wanting to look like a professor. No need to feel embarrassed."

"Embarrassed? I'm just trying to measure up to my beautiful wife."

Now it was her turn to blush. After he left, she imagined him reciting lines of poetry as he drove to the university, working to get the inflection just so. She smiled at the thought of him working at his craft just as she worked at hers.

Back then, Cole had been proud of his wife. Called her "soldering-gun Picasso." And when she became pregnant, he suggested that she give up her job.

"I can provide for the two of us," he'd said, running his hands over her growing belly. "You should follow your passion."

The life of a full-time mother, wife, and artist appealed to her. All the passion she needed was right here at home. "I might just do that," she answered.

"Excuse me." The man from the next table was standing by her chair. "My son is fascinated by your necklace. He bet me you made it yourself."

Marty looked at him, her face a barrier.

"He wants to make jewelry. Already has an internship with a jeweler, and he's only fourteen. Join us for dessert?"

"Not tonight, thanks." *Stay on your side; don't cross here.*

"As a favor to my son. Please." He put one hand on the table and folded his body down until the two of them were almost eye level. She rose, and as she followed him, a gentle movement of the ship reminded Marty how her belly had rippled during her pregnancy whenever her daughter had changed positions.

Pregnancy had been magical for Marty—a time when her senses overflowed their boundaries, and her baby's heartbeats fluttered a message only she could hear. "You are a part of me, and I will always love you." She and Cole laughed at the undulating geography of her body and decided to name the baby Lana because it sounded like velvet and meant calm-as-still-water in Hawaiian. Later, cradling Lana on her lap, Marty sang her daughter's heartbeats back to her in a lullaby.

Lana was the kind of child everyone wanted to cuddle. With the exception of a few rare tantrums, her temperament reflected her name. Cole would tell her, "If you were a weather report, I'd call you sunny with a chance of thunderstorms." Once when she was five, she tapped Marty on the shoulder. "You look sad, Mommy, so I made you a Valentine's card even though it's not Valentine's Day." That lace-trimmed construction paper heart still hung in her studio.

Marty's work-at-home schedule meant she was there with milk and cookies when Lana came home from school. She drove her to playdates, watched her march in the elementary school Halloween parade, chaperoned class trips, and helped out in the classroom when needed. And she had time alone in her basement studio to pursue her craft. Marty worked slowly, and each completed piece felt like a kind of birth. At first, she was reluctant to sell her "babies," but letting go of them became easier in time.

On his days off, Cole morphed into a milk-and-cookie dad, which delighted Lana. He played games with her and helped with homework. As he took on more academic responsibilities in pursuit of tenure, he had less time to spend with Lana, making the little time they had together more precious to her. Marty loved watching the two of them together. So many of Cole's male colleagues gave short shrift to their wives and families as they pursued their academic goals, and she was proud to have a husband who, though ambitious, wasn't all about work.

Marty jammed the heaviest pieces into the pockets of her hiking pants, adding an antique bronze ashtray for more weight. She hoped the loose fit would provide cover. She was running out of outfits, out of time.

"Are you nervous, Cole?" asked Marty, stringing another bead on the nylon cord of her half-finished necklace.

Cole closed the literary journal he was reading and leaned back against the sofa cushion. "A little. I've been working six years for this."

Marty reached into the bead box on the table next to her chair. "I can't imagine why you wouldn't get it. You've published, and the students adore you." The beads clattered like a baby's rattle.

"And I play their political games like a pro." His fingers imitated a pair of flapping lips.

"Cole, you've never doubted yourself, so why start now?"

"Come over here," he said.

She put the unfinished necklace on the table and sat next to him on the couch. He took her hand in both of his and ran his thumb along the silver coils of her bracelet. She looked at his long delicate fingers with their chewed nails. He never appeared concerned about his academic future, but his fingernails told a different story.

He walked to the stereo and turned up the music, a jazz version of "Favorite Things."

He gently steered her to the middle of the room. As they rocked back and forth, the fingers of his left hand kneaded her back. "Tomorrow. Tenure. Everything," he whispered. "Biggest day of my life." He lowered his right hand and gently, for seconds that seemed like minutes, squeezed her butt.

"Cole," she said softly, "Lana's at the top of the stairs, watching."

He chuckled and repositioned his hand on her waist. "Later," he whispered.

"Mommy, Daddy, can I dance with you?"

"It's late, sweetie," Cole called up the steps. "Go back to bed." Then softly to Marty, "Let's give it an hour, then do the same."

He pulled her closer.

The next night, Cole was late getting home, but Marty wasn't worried. She figured he was probably out celebrating, though she was surprised he didn't call. Lana wanted to stay up and wait for him, so Marty had read her three stories before she finally fell asleep. She changed into her nightgown, got into bed, and realized it was ten o'clock. Must be quite a celebration. She was about to turn out the light when the front door slammed.

"Marty," yelled Cole. She could hear his heavy footsteps on the stairs. "*Marty!*"

She turned on the light as he strode into the room. "Sssh," she said softly. "Lana's asleep."

"I didn't get it. Someone in the department must have had it in for me," he yelled. "I'll find out who, swear to God, and kill the fucker." His face distorted with rage. Who was this man? He picked up a book from the nightstand and threw it against the wall. Marty jumped. She knew he had a temper, had heard him cursing from time to time when he worked in his study, but he'd never lost it in her presence. His actions must have shocked him as much as her, because when he turned to her, the rage was gone. He picked the book up and examined it for damage. "I'm sorry," he said, and she wasn't sure whether he was talking to her, or to the book.

"What happened?"

"They told me my published work wasn't 'robust' enough, whatever that means."

"What happens now?"

"I have a year to appeal. I'm going to work like hell to write something that will get everyone's attention. Work to get everyone on my side."

The next day he went about his business as if nothing had happened, but as time passed she sensed that something had changed, that he was no longer the Cole she'd married. There was a hard, clench-jawed edge to him. Sometimes he looked past Marty, erasing her, eyes focused on the only prize worth winning: tenure. At other times, he looked at her with an expression she couldn't fathom, as if she were the one who had changed. She remembered the class she'd attended where the girls worshipped him like a god.

As far as she knew, Cole had never experienced academic failure, from his straight-A school days to his summa cum laude graduation from an Ivy League university, to the dissertation that was praised and published the first year they were married. Academia had been smooth sailing for him, but the tide had suddenly shifted. It occurred to her that his uninterrupted success had not prepared him for the inevitable failure everyone experiences at least once in a lifetime.

Over the next few months, Marty tried to get used to the new Cole, who spent days at the office and nights in his study. She enjoyed the extra time with Lana and was able to spend more time in her studio and take jewelry classes. Her teacher encouraged her to exhibit her pieces at the art center, and to her surprise and delight, they sold. She created a website and gained a following. Her sales increased, enabling her to purchase more expensive materials, like gold and precious stones, which raised her profile and her profits.

As she grew as an artist, Cole spent more and more time away from home. It was as if he'd found a new family of colleagues to cultivate and seminar students to spearhead a campaign to protest his tenure denial. Occasionally he integrated his two "families," inviting colleagues over for dinner. He seemed to make special efforts to show the dinner guests what a good family man he was. Show them how he supported his wife and was not a chauvinist.

He made it a point to compliment her work. "Look at that, Kenner," he said to a friend of his in the department, pointing to the multicolored knotted rope necklace Marty was wearing. "Isn't that something. She made that. Posted a photo on her website a couple days ago and sold five of them, just like that." Larry Kenner was sitting next to his wife, but his eyes lingered a bit too long on her breasts. No one else seemed to notice.

When there were no guests, Cole's reaction to her work was tepid at best. She showed him the bracelet she planned to submit to a prestigious art competition—fifty small pieces of gold forged and folded and soldered together in intricate patterns and embedded with opals—and he reacted with a "very nice" that could have been machine generated. He berated her for spending so much time with her business instead of helping him. When she asked how she could help, he shrugged his shoulders. She couldn't figure out what he wanted from her.

Some nights he and Marty made love violently, as if she were on an opposing team. Other nights, alone in bed, she wondered whether he was secretly measuring his success against hers, resenting her growth as an artist while he struggled to keep his job, because if he didn't get tenure, he'd probably have to move on to a different college, which to him was the ultimate slap in the face. "It doesn't matter who earns more money," he insisted. But did he believe that? Did any man?

The gold bracelet she'd submitted for competition won an award of distinction and a four-figure cash prize, and they invited her to attend the conference and award ceremony in Miami. While she was in Florida, Cole called to tell her his final application for tenure had been denied. She knew that academic politics were cutthroat and the administration was always trying to save money by hiring adjunct professors, but he couldn't, or wouldn't, tell her why he'd been denied. She offered to come home.

"Don't cut your trip short," he said, sounding unnaturally calm. "You won an award. Celebrate. I've scheduled vacation time and canceled the babysitter, so I'll be here when Lana gets home from school."

She wanted to get home, be a family, but he insisted she stay where she was.

Marty sat across the table from the man and the boy, who looked younger than fourteen, with his cowlicky hair and vulnerable face. When the man told her he was newly divorced and had joint custody, the boy's lips formed a tight line. *Lucky you. Divorced is still-could-be. Dead is engraved-in-stone.* She half-listened as he told her they'd been visiting his aunt and uncle in Turkey. Once they got back to New York, he explained, the boy would fly to the West Coast to live with his mother. The boy turned his face to the window.

Anxious to leave, Marty turned the conversation back to the topic that had brought her to the table. "Your father tells me you're interested in jewelry."

The boy turned back, his face all color, all child. "I bet he didn't tell you I'm studying geology, too. You take rocks and make, like, a necklace. Some lady buys it, passes it on to her daughter, who passes it on to her daughter. Or the person dies and wears it when she's buried. Either way, it's recycled. So, I'm an artist and an ecologist all in one." He smiled. "That's an awesome piece you're wearing. You make it? Can I see?" Marty half stood and leaned over the table, holding the necklace out toward him. The boy reached out, and she watched his fingers trace the contours of the freshwater pearls embedded like stars in multiple silver strands of her necklace. "It looks like the universe," he said.

On the back of a cocktail napkin, the boy illustrated the first piece he'd ever made. It was a miniature puzzle pin, interlocking copper slices on a silver backing. As he described the way the pin could be disassembled and reassembled "like a real puzzle," he said, his face lit up like a proud new papa. There was a completeness to the work, as if it were his grand finale, though it was only the beginning for him. She complimented him on his ingenuity.

Crack of onyx on tile. Her hands shook as she bent down to grab the stone. Before stuffing it into her oversized bra, she rubbed the smooth surface, remembering how she'd been drawn to the textures of her craft, the ways they echoed the human condition—the softness of skin on skin, the hardness of human heart. When she dropped the onyx into the cup of her bra, it clinked against the other stones.

It was a gradual process—the shifting of affections. Soon after Marty returned from the conference, she was cleaning out the upstairs linen closet when she heard laughter and scraps of conversation drifting up from the living room. From the top of the stairs, she could see Cole and Lana playing *Monopoly* on the floor. An ice cream truck outside looped its endless melody.

"Dance with me, Daddy."

"Sure, baby." He picked up two plastic houses and danced them around the board.

Lana nudged him with her elbow. "You're silly." Then she grabbed a hotel off Boardwalk and imitated her father. Neither of them noticed Marty at the top of the stairs. She told herself she was staying upstairs to give them more father-daughter time, but the truth was that Cole subtly discouraged her inclusion, turning his back to her when the three of them were together, or talking over her. It was as if he'd shifted his competitive focus from academia to parenting; if he couldn't be the big-shot professor, he could be the perfect dad.

The undermining of her authority, like the shifting of affections, happened gradually and was well established by the time Lana was a teenager. There was the argument they'd had about the tattoo Lana wanted to get.

"It's only a tattoo, Marty. A butterfly."

"Did you see what she wants to get? The size of it? It'll start on her butt and run halfway up her back. A neon sign: 'Come see my ass.'"

"Which her clothes will cover."

"Low-rise jeans don't cover crap."

Lana came to their bedroom door and stood watching them go at it.

"You're making too big a deal."

"She's only fourteen."

"Like fourteen isn't old enough," Lana broke in. "You had your ears pierced when you were fourteen. Your parents were freaked."

"She has a point, Marty."

"Dammit, Cole. This isn't about me. It's about our daughter. And what's appropriate at her age." It had become a familiar two-against-one choreography. "Who's the parent here, Cole?" Marty turned away from Cole and slammed her fist into the palm of her other hand, as tears filled her eyes. Marty felt like she'd lost them both. She considered divorce, but felt she had a better chance of getting through to her husband and daughter if she stayed.

When she ran into Larry Kenner at a nearby Starbucks and he eyed her with interest, she met his gaze. She nourished herself with the hope that things could change. But when she was sleepless at three o'clock in the morning, Marty feared that nothing was going to change.

I still need more weight, she thought, slipping a glass paperweight into the pocket of her raincoat. Then she grabbed a bronze Buddha figurine off the shelf for good measure. That should do it.

As Marty left the dining room with the man and the boy, the ship rolled and Marty felt the steadying touch of the man's hand on her shoulder. Marty silently rehearsed her getaway lines. When they passed through the dining room door into the lobby, the boy said he was going to the game room. Marty extended her hand to him, but he stood looking at her, face unreadable. Then, moving a step closer, the boy put his arms around her, burying his face in her neck. His hair smelled like citrus, and she could feel the not-quite-man chest under his silk shirt. Tentatively, she put an arm around him, and they stood locked, as if she were the missing puzzle piece in his life. Then the boy slipped out of her arms and walked off. The man watched his son go, his face a canvas of longing.

When the boy was out of sight, the man turned to her. "I'm heading over to the ballroom later. Would you come with me? For an hour?" His look was pleading.

An hour of companionship, she thought. Why not? Tomorrow he'll be somewhere in Greece, and I'll be gone. I've already written the note and put it in my stateroom on the nightstand, so they won't have to search the ship for me. I won't leave Lana a legacy of uncertainty or guilt, like Cole left me.

The note explained that her mother's suicide wasn't Lana's fault—that Lana had just been a victim of her parents' demons—and she begged her daughter's forgiveness. I'll have a quiet passing, she thought. A dance, a splash, then nothing but the lights on shore. A final dance, then...

"Yes," she answered. "I'll dance with you."

It had been years since her husband had held her.

When Lana was fifteen, Marty had taken her to a mall. Marty had stopped to look at something in a window while Lana walked ahead. When Marty looked up, she saw a butt-swinging, spiky-haired stranger in the distance and realized it was her daughter. How had this happened? She remembered a line from a song: *You were so much mine, now I reach for you and I cannot find you.*

Marty had tried to break through to her original daughter, the sweet-girl memory, the five-year-old who'd handed Marty a Valentine's card one April morning because her mommy looked so sad. But nothing in her maternal toolkit could penetrate the anger that had hardened her daughter.

The man held her at the waist—a prelude to nothing. There was space between them, no eye contact, as her feet moved to muscle memory. The man pulled her close as if to embrace. Marty pulled back and he stumbled, but he righted himself as he maintained his grip on her. He lowered his mouth to her ear: "My wife left me, said she hated me, hated my family. Was glad they're dead." She realized he held her tight so his pain wouldn't flatten him. They clung to each other in grief.

Marty had known something was wrong as soon as she walked into the house. It wasn't five o'clock yet, and Cole was home with a stack of papers on his lap.

"Why so early? What's wrong?"

Silence.

"What's wrong?"

"Wrong?" he mimicked her voice as he stood up. "I ran into a colleague this morning. Said he saw you at the Marriott a few weeks ago. He told me he wanted to say hello, when he saw Larry Kenner come up behind you. Saw! You and Larry-fucking-Kenner get on the elevator. Probably something innocent, he told me. Wasn't planning to say anything. Just slipped out."

In a low voice: "Slipped out, my ass. Enjoyed every word, the prick."

Marty hadn't been attracted to Larry, but he must have sensed her vulnerability and worked it. Their Starbucks encounter led to two afternoons in a rented bed and the realization that another man's hands on her body wouldn't heal her. So she'd ended it months earlier.

"Was he good in bed, Marty?"

Marty's voice was locked in her throat.

"Any new tricks he can teach me? Come on, sweetheart, I wanna hear all the freaking details."

"You haven't touched me in months."

"You're always at those goddamn craft shows."

"I'm home almost every night."

"I'm drowning in work shit, and you couldn't wait till the pressure was off me. Had to screw my friend. No wonder I'm not getting anywhere. You're the freaking albatross around my neck."

Marty looked to the top of the stairs to see if Lana was there. She wasn't, not yet anyway. But she could probably hear every word from her bedroom.

"Let her *hear* her mother's a whore. I can't believe you did this to me. All those girls in my classes itching to fuck me. Every day! And I never touched one." There were tears in his eyes, on his cheeks. "I shoulda fucked 'em all. Taught 'em real poetry." He grabbed his car keys and headed for the door. "I'm outta here."

Sitting on the sofa later that evening, dizzy and slightly nauseous, Marty heard a timid knock at the door. *Was it him?* Her heart raced with anxiety as she contemplated what lay ahead for the two of them. More knocking, louder this time. *He must have forgotten his key.* She exhaled sharply before lifting herself from the sofa and making her way to the door. Her eyes widened when she found herself facing a tall young man in a deep blue uniform and cap. He said something, but the words didn't register. She stepped back to let him in.

"Ma'am," he said, removing his cap to reveal a blond buzz cut.

Now her heart was pounding. She knew what was coming. "Would you like a glass of water?

He shook his head. "Perhaps you'd like to sit down."

"You're sure you don't want something to drink?" she said, delaying the inevitable as long as possible.

Again he shook his head. "I'm so sorry ma'am. Your husband..."

She lowered herself onto the nearest chair.

"Your husband was in an accident. His car ran into a tree. He ... he didn't make it. I'm so sorry."

"*You killed him. You killed my dad!*" The shriek from the top of the steps startled Marty and the officer. The young man shook his head and shrugged, hands inarticulate, absurd as lobster claws. He waited till the shouting stopped. A woman sitting on her porch saw it all, he told her. "She said he was driving erratically and speeding, like he was drunk."

Cole wasn't a drinker, and Marty knew it was fury, not alcohol, that had fueled this accident.

The officer told her the particulars—where they'd taken his body, what she needed to do.

"*You killed him,*" Lana yelled again after the officer left.

Marty wandered from room to room, touching objects no longer familiar, brushing against walls so insubstantial she could have walked through them. She was afraid the weight of her body would send her through the floor.

She went upstairs and found Lana beating her fist against the windowsill in her bedroom, tears streaming.

"Baby—"

Lana's fist gaveled judgment. "Not. Your. Baby. You treat me like a baby. Dad and I talk all the time about how you treat me."

"You and your father talked? About me?"

"He calls your rules shit."

He sabotaged me all along. I never stood a chance. If he weren't dead, I'd kill him.

"What am I going to do?" Lana sobbed. "He's the only one that understands me. You don't have a clue." Lana sucked in her lower lip, as if eating the mouth that had robbed her of her self-control—the mouth of a kid who knew she'd gone too far but couldn't stop.

"You're killing me," Marty whispered, barely able to catch her breath, her words dissipating like vapor.

"*You* killed *him*!"

"I…he was angry. You know your father's temper. He lost it, got in the car, and—"

"Don't blame him." Lana's face was crimson. "Blame yourself."

"Stop it!" Marty clutched her long, beaded necklace, a perfect noose.

"I'll say whatever I want. He loved me more than you, so you fucked that creep. Probably fucked a bunch of creeps."

She twisted the necklace and it broke, glass beads smacking against the hardwood floor. Marty stepped back, twisting her ankle on a loose stone. As she fell, Lana instinctively reached out to help her but quickly pulled back, watching her mother fall and swallowing the "Mommy!" that had started to slip out.

Marty staggered out of the room, and Lana slammed the door. Sometime during the night, Lana left the house and didn't return. Two days later, Marty got a call from her sister in California.

"Lana's here. I'm sure this isn't permanent."

"You don't believe that any more than I do," said Marty before she ended the call.

After she said goodbye to the man, she returned to her stateroom. She pulled everything she needed out of her heavy suitcase and laid it on the bed. She put on the baggy pants, fisherman's vest, and baggy raincoat. Then she filled the pockets with jewelry and knickknacks as she'd practiced. There were some loose pieces that jangled in the raincoat pockets, so she stuffed washcloths into the two pockets. She opened the door and checked the corridor before taking the back steps to the floor with access to the walking deck.

The common area was empty except for a couple sitting at a café table on the far side of the room. Marty ducked back into the corridor and waited for them to leave before approaching the door that opened onto the deck. She pulled the handle down and pushed against it with her body until it opened with a whoosh. Once on deck, she slipped off her heels and shivered as her feet made contact with the cold, wet planks. Though it was summer, the air was chilly, and the movement of the ship challenged her equilibrium. As she made her way to the railing, the sharp contours of her jewelry-lined clothing cut into her flesh. *My life's work turned psycho.*

She held onto the railing with one hand, and her free hand brushed something rough against her raincoat. Her beaded shoulder bag. She bent her arm and slid her thumb under the strap of her evening bag to lift it away from her shoulder.

An albatross around his neck. "Water, water everywhere," Cole would singsong when he quoted the poet for whom he was named. Marty released the strap and let it slide down her arm. The bag was nearly empty, hanging lightly from her wrist before slipping off onto the deck. The suicide note! She'd intended to leave it on the nightstand of her cabin, but there it was, her final words to her daughter, stuck in her ridiculous beaded handbag. The ship tilted ever so slightly, and a gust of wind washed the bag overboard. Without a note to leave behind, she would be burdening Lana with the possibility that she might have been responsible for her mother's death. Much as Marty longed for the release of oblivion, she could not put such a weight on her child's shoulders.

The lights on the shoreline danced as the ship sailed on into the night. As she stood suspended between two continents, she replayed the man's anguished words, and she remembered the boy's arms tightening around her, the feel of his ribs against her chest. Anchor me for just a moment, his body had said. Just a moment before they send me away.

A door opened somewhere, and a trill of laughter dissipated into the night air like the evanescent flicker of starlight. Marty envied the weightlessness of the night sky and the shore lights that grew fainter as the channel widened into the Aegean. She reached into her pocket and pulled out a heavy jade bracelet that sparkled as it caught the overhead light. She was about to release it, to unburden herself of all her creations—of everything—but was stopped by a memory: the aching power of the boy's need and the potency of her embrace, which had comforted him.

She put the bracelet back in her pocket, fished around for the paperweight, and dropped it overboard, watching as it slipped silently into the void. She did the same with the two bronze pieces, feeling lighter with each piece she relinquished. And when she had nothing more to surrender, she turned and went back inside.

ManFred's Other Cheek

ManFred gave a victory hoot as he watched the news crawl past at the bottom of the television screen. *Subway riders to drop pants in global event.* There it was, on CNN. Next Friday at noon, the world would see the largest display of anatomical posteriority in history, thanks to him. He updated his Facebook status to describe the coming event as "a flash mob bigger than the What Would Elvis Do dance party in Vatican Square and even bigger than the Hokey-Pokeython in lower Manhattan." Yes, ManFred would show everyone, especially his archrival, what he could do.

Even as a child, ManFred, né Freddie Finsterman, had grandiose artistic ambitions. For a fifth grade art project, he'd sprinkled glitter on three of his friends and glued them together. At thirteen, Freddie had changed his name to ManFred in emulation of the single-name artists he so admired: Cher, Picasso, Bono, Coco, and his future mentor-turned-tormentor, CaCa.

CaCa (né Carlos Caramillio) was an experimental artist best known for his Bodily Fluids exhibit, which was proclaimed a masterpiece by *The New York Times* and praised for its innovative use of excrement by *Time Magazine*. When he saw ManFred's sculpture of a three-hundred-pound woman carved out of hamburger buns at the New School, CaCa pulled him aside.

"You're quite talented. How would you like to team up?" He placed a fatherly hand on the young man's shoulder. CaCa would later admit that he knew he was way more talented than ManFred but figured that partnering with a rising star could only help his career.

"I'd be honored," ManFred answered, speaking with the deference of an acolyte.

Their first collaboration was an exhibition pairing the bun lady with a wagonload of McDonald's hamburgers. The Empty Calories, Big Buns exhibit at MOMA, was a huge success, and a legendary partnership was born. Inspired by conceptual artist Christo, the two wrapped the state of Wyoming in aluminum foil. The art world was dazzled, so when the Whitney Biennial rejected their Pain Schmain project, CaCa was stunned.

"How could they nix a live appendectomy?"

"They're heartless. Let's put it on YouTube."

So it was that ManFred introduced his mentor to social media—a decision that would prove fateful for the young artist.

In the eyes of the world, the two artists were getting along smashingly, though each had secretly hired his own agent. Then came the opening of the Kitty Litter exhibit at the Guggenheim; each artist insisted his name be listed first.

"*My* work."

"*My* idea."

"Derivative."

"Insipid."

Insults flew like paintballs, and they parted company, each vowing to publicly humiliate and outdo the other.

CaCa hired his ten-year-old nephew, Timmy, to brief him

on social media. Timmy set him up on Twitter and Facebook, and within days, @CaCaTheArtist had a million and a half followers, and #ManFredSucks was trending.

ManFred was striking back with the pants-down extravaganza. He advertised his upcoming event on billboards across the country: *Get ready! It's coming Friday, July 12. Visit ManFred.com.* He appeared on all the late-night talk shows and got laughs on *Letterman* with his tagline: *CaCa—his name says it all.*

ManFred was too busy with his own projects to pay attention to his rival's online activities on social media, so he missed CaCa's tweets announcing the launch of something hot hot hot.

On the day of the pants-down event, ManFred staked out a spot in Times Square. A crowd gathered around him. At the appointed hour, he loosened his belt and pulled down his pants. But everyone standing with him reach for their smartphones instead of their pants.

"What's going on?" ManFred asked a nearby woman whose thumbs were moving a mile a minute.

"It's the Sex Drive. Everybody has one." As ManFred pulled up his pants, the woman told him how that CaCa had partnered with a rogue Microsoft programmer to develop a revolutionary new technology—multi-sensory online pornography. The app was downloaded by millions of people and launched at noon. The promotional campaign had promised to give new meaning to the term "touch screen." She told him that millions had laughed at his clever online advertising featuring spokes-dolls Animated Barbie ("Still anatomically impossible and proud of it") and the new, improved Ken ("Now with genitalia!").

ManFred staggered into a Starbucks just as his cell phone sounded the urgent-message ringtone. He opened the message and dropped the phone when an image of CaCa's bare butt filled the screen.

Devastated by his adversary's public victory, ManFred picked up a can of spray paint and went underground. Now his work appears only on the walls and ceilings of subway stops up and down the Sixth Avenue line. But ManFred is determined to rise again. He tags his work Still-the-ManFred, and he's working on a project he promises will wipe out his rival. He won't reveal much, except to say he'll be using a lot of Charmin.

Monovision

amned Pine Barrens roads all look alike. I turned down another Jersey-flat country road just as the sun teased the tops of the pines on its downward journey. There was still time to find my mother's favorite vintage shop near Hammonton—or was it Batsto—before nightfall. I couldn't think of a better birthday present for her than a piece of over-sized costume jewelry—the more rhinestones, the better. Her birthday was tomorrow, so this was the only opportunity I had to locate her favorite second-hand shop.

My phone was out of juice, which meant no GPS. If I still used maps, I'd have been able to read the tiny print with my new progressive lenses. The optometrist had diagnosed me with monovision, a condition where one eye is nearsighted and the other farsighted. When I was younger, she explained, I could keep the world in balance by subconsciously switching focus thousands of times a day; but my farsighted eye had gradually grown stronger and the myopic one weaker, so at age thirty-nine I had to succumb to the inevitable. I got my first pair of glasses.

I frowned at the empty road ahead and clutched the locket that hung from a chain on my neck. As I slid it back and forth along the chain, the familiar ratchety sound soothed me. The locket had been a gift from my father, whom I'd never met, as far as I knew; as I ran my thumb over my engraved initials, GG, I tried to conjure up his presence. All I knew was this: His name was Albert Bishop, he was an only child, and he was killed in Vietnam when I was two years old. When I was little, I wasn't afraid to question my mother, Rose, about him.

"Did he ever meet me?"

"Of course, Grace. He gave you that locket, didn't he?

"Why didn't you marry someone else after he died?"

"Albert was the love of my life. You'll understand when you grow up. Believe me."

I believed her. How could I not have? Rose was my best friend—my extroverted, bigger-than-life mother, who insisted I call her by her first name so she wouldn't feel so old. She revealed almost nothing about my father, but had no problem talking to me about things other kids had to learn from magazines and videos stashed away in their parents' nightstands, underneath the Bibles and the moisturizing cream. On school holidays, Rose took me to her beauty salon on Passyunk Avenue, where she permed, colored, manicured, and gossiped with the ladies, who adored her. Afterward, she'd swear me to secrecy before sharing juicy bits and pieces of their lives, like how Mrs. Rossi's husband was cheating on her, and how Mrs. Pagano's "homemade" cake actually came from Termini's Bakery. When I was old enough to read the pain in her eyes whenever I asked about my father, I stopped asking. Making Rose happy had become a focus of my life back then—still was, I guess—which was why I was going out of my way to find her the perfect gift.

I folded up the useless map and put it back in the door pocket. I'd give myself five more minutes to drive around before heading back to Philly, where I could hopefully squeeze in a quick visit with Rose at the Oakwood Manor Retirement Community. Turning down yet another copycat road, I spotted a gray clapboard storefront set back in a thicket of pines.

The roof had missing tiles, and the pitted siding had a mottled look, as if it had lost a fistfight. The freshly painted "Vinny's Vintage" sign looked a bit garish in such shabby surroundings. This wasn't the secondhand shop I'd been looking for, but it looked promising. And maybe someone in there would be able to tell me the quickest route back to Philly.

The inside of Vinny's was a kaleidoscopic jumble of mid-twentieth century bits and pieces. The proprietor was a skinny old guy. He looked like an auto mechanic, in his white shirt with *Vinny* embroidered in red on the pocket.

"Howdy," he said with a smile. "Looking for anything special?"

"I'll know it when I see it." I smiled back. "Do you have any costume jewelry?"

"Yup. Last row." He pointed.

Grabbing a plastic shopping basket to hold my finds, I made my way down an aisle lined with towering shelves of dusty discards—*I Love Lucy* memorabilia, white kid gloves, rotary phones, princess phones, Bakelite dishes—everything but jewelry. I thought Vinny must have been mistaken about the aisle, but at the very end sat a wicker basket of costume jewelry. I sorted through the disappointingly small collection of pins, brooches, earrings, and necklaces but couldn't find anything sufficiently Rose-like. Not wanting to leave empty-handed, I settled on an antique snake bracelet that wrapped twice around the wrist. The snake had green gemstone eyes. That would do if I couldn't find something better.

I moved on to another aisle, to a collection of perfume bottles made of antique cut glass, hand-painted and gilded. I pulled out glass stoppers, releasing faint traces of the fragrances the bottles had once held. A cobalt blue bottle, less ornate than the others, yielded a citrusy scent that somehow reminded me of my father, though it was obviously a false memory. I'd been far too young when he died to remember anything about him. But the association was strong. I replaced the stopper and gently placed the bottle in my basket.

At the end of the aisle I bumped into a coat rack hung with scarves. One scarf, a length of silky fabric, slid onto the floor, forming a fluorescent pool of pink, orange, and fuchsia. A scarf that clashed with itself—the perfect birthday gift for Rose. I slipped it into my basket and headed for the checkout counter.

Vinnie rang up the scarf and then studied my face. "Those glasses you're wearing. They was made for you."

I touched the blue translucent frames of my progressives. "Thanks."

Vinny was kind of cute for an old guy. Great head of white hair. Maybe he'd make a better gift for Rose than the scarf. "Nah, too skinny," Rose would say. "I like 'em with handles."

I asked Vinny for directions to the Walt Whitman Bridge. He drew a crude map on the back of a paper Santa placemat and handed it to me.

Outside, the sun had dipped behind the pines. The cold mid-December air stung my cheeks, but I lingered a moment to enjoy the quiet. Viewed through the upper half of my lenses, the scene was photorealistic, as if each pine needle had been etched with a stylus. Then I tilted my head back slightly to view the same scene through the lower half of the lenses, and my surroundings were transformed into an impressionistic landscape, the same blurred view I'd gotten used to before my vision was corrected. As I walked to my car, I noticed a particular tree. Though the leaves were gone, I recognized the peeling bark of a sycamore tree—a lone sycamore in the land of pines. There had been a sycamore in front of our row house on Porter Street, where we'd moved when I was four. I remembered peeling the bark, worrying that I might be hurting the tree but unable to stop. My mother would often scold me for how much I cared. "Gracie, you're too damned sensitive. Always afraid you'll hurt someone's feelings."

Thanks to Vinnie's map, I made it to Oakwood Manor in time. I waited outside the dining room for Rose to finish dinner, my heavy jacket draped over my arm. I noticed a comma-curved lady in a pink tracksuit leaning against her walker.

She stood looking at a painted mural showing a South Philly street, with a block of neat brick row houses. There were store-fronts with green awnings on each corner, and a park on the next block was visible at the edge of the mural. A meatloafy-cabbage smell gave a hint of what Rose and the others were eating. Soon, wheelchairs were rolling out of the dining room. The woman was still standing in front of the mural. Her hand shook as she pulled a purple marker out of a nearby box. With her tongue peeking out between her lips, she printed two sets of initials on a park bench. Then she put the marker back in the box and blew a kiss at the bench.

I smiled. That mural would never have come to be without my mother. And my mother wouldn't have come to be at Oakwood if she hadn't broken both her hips. She was only seventy-one, but it turned out that fractured femurs were a rare side effect of the osteoporosis medication she'd been taking. The popular drug that was supposed to strengthen her bones ended up breaking them. The bones didn't heal completely, and Rose knew she could no longer live alone, but she fought against going to a senior community. "I ain't old enough for no old age home," she told me. I offered to have her live with me and my daughter—we had an extra bedroom. But she insisted she didn't want to be a burden. Finally, when I assured her that we'd find a continuing-care community where she'd have her own apartment, she gave in. "Just tell them I'm going to liven up the joint," she said. And she did.

When I'd moved Rose into Oakwood Manor, the wall that was now covered by the mural had been white. Comma Lady, a fellow South Philly native who lived down the hall from Rose, had told Rose how much she missed the old neighborhood. Their shared nostalgia motivated my mother to supervise the creation of a mural of South Philly. She collected memories from former row-home residents, memories of corner stores and Breyer's ice-cream signs, and she made sure the artist got them right. When he'd finished, Rose painted in a Passyunk Avenue street sign, a woman sweeping her stoop, and a girl playing hopscotch. She asked the staff to keep a supply of Magic Markers on hand so residents could add their own real or imagined memories. "There's plenty of wall space left to fill," she told them, "and I hate white space."

Comma Lady turned and saw me looking at her. "He was my first love," she explained, tilting her head toward the park bench with the initials. "Dumped me in eighth grade." She swiveled the walker and bumped her way down the hall.

I walked over to the nurse's station, where Lizzy, a tall, thin African-American woman with elaborate hair extensions, was sitting. She'd been on duty the first time we'd visited Oakwood, when Rose had remarked that she liked the place, "but it needs more color."

"You're right about that," Lizzy had answered. The two of them had laughed, and it hadn't taken long for them to become buddies. For the Fourth of July, Rose gave Lizzy a colorful red-white-and-blue manicure, and that sealed the friendship.

I asked Lizzy why my mother hadn't exited the dining room, and she answered that Rose and her friends had lost track of time playing cards and were late coming down to dinner.

"They're just finishing their dinner," Lizzy said. "Why don't you just go in?"

"Nah, I don't want to disturb them. I'll just wait for her in her room. Don't tell her I'm here. I want to surprise her."

I rode the elevator upstairs to the independent living wing and walked down the hall to Rose's one-bedroom. Like many residents, my mother left the door unlocked when she went to dinner. They didn't keep valuable items in their apartments. Once inside, I laid my jacket over the back of a loveseat that served as a sofa in the small living room and sat down in one of the wingback chairs that she'd brought with her. I checked my emails on my phone and looked at the time. Still no Rose. She should be back by now, I thought, a little worried; then I remembered how much she loved to schmooze with the residents and staff. I checked out the knickknacks in Rose's old display cabinet. The shelves were only half-full, which was partially my fault. I'd promised her I'd stop by the storage facility and get the rest of them, but with a full-time job and a daughter, I never seemed to find the time. This day was a rare day off for me.

I wandered over to the gallery of framed photographs that hung on the opposite wall. There were black-and-white photos of Rose growing up, and color photos of me and of my daughter, Zoe. None with my ex-husband—she must have put those in a drawer, for which I was grateful. And there were pictures of the "uncles," which is how she referred to the men in her life. The centerpiece of the display was a black-and-white photo of my father standing on the beach, his arm around my mother, staring at something in the distance. I liked to imagine he was staring at me.

I focused on his face. This photo had hung in my mother's bedroom at our Porter Street row house when I was little. I must have spent hours in front of that photo, sucking my thumb as I stroked the red and black flocked wallpaper. I have no memory of my father—only of the feel of red velvet against my fingers and this photograph. Leaning in closer, I looked for something of myself in his features but couldn't see a resemblance. My hair was dark and curly like my mother's, and his was straight and blond. My face was round, his angular. Why hadn't I noticed that before?

I studied the faces of the men I had called uncles; it was only when I was older that my mother had hinted that they weren't blood relatives. Did I look like "Uncle" Bernie? A little, around the eyes. Could *he* be my father—Uncle Bernie, who'd pulled quarters out of my ears, his hair smelling of some product no one wears anymore? What about "Uncle" Mac, a big man who smoked Cuban cigars? I remembered him lifting me onto his shoulders to see the clowns in the New Year's parade. Did I look anything like him? I scanned the gallery of colorful men.

As far as I knew, none of the uncles had stayed overnight. But I couldn't imagine my mother remaining celibate all those years. A woman like Rose Giordano—life of the party, bawdy, sexy, exuberant Rose Giordano—must have found ways to share her ample gifts when I wasn't around. It was a possibility I hadn't considered until I became a single parent and learned to appreciate the lengths to which a mother would go to shield her children from intimacies with men who weren't their fathers.

"Gracie, what are you doin' here? What's wrong? I wasn't expectin' you till tomorrow for my birthday." Rose stood in the doorway, leaning on her walker. For a moment, she looked older than her almost seventy-two years, a single mother, like me, who had sacrificed so much for her only child.

I walked to the doorway and hugged her. "Everything's okay. I was just going to stop by and say hi. But I can't wait to show you your birthday present."

"A present!" She stood straighter, and her face was all child. "Give me a minute to sit down. It's a pisser when your body flips you the bird." She picked up the cane hanging from the walker and hobbled over to a wingback chair identical to the one I was sitting in.

"Didn't the doctor tell you to wait a couple more weeks before you started with a cane? Remember what happened three months ago, when you were in such a hurry after the surgeries that you reinjured one of your hips?"

"Honey, I gotta exercise. Otherwise I'll get as fat as a cannoli." Rose lowered herself into the chair and adjusted her sweater, a blue cardigan with pink appliquéd flowers that were the exact color of her pants. A gold chain belt hung loosely around her waist. Rose had written in her living will that she wanted to go to her grave fully accessorized. "So, where's my present?"

I pulled the scarf out of my bag and held it to the side, waving it matador style. The perfume bottle was in my bag, too, and I could smell the cologne when I got the scarf out. Apparently, so could she.

"Nice perfume," she said without showing any emotion. I'd obviously been mistaken about the scent's connection to my father. Then she put her attention on the scarf. "Oh, Gracie, it's beautiful. Put it on me, would ya?"

I knelt in front of her, and as I draped the scarf around the back of her neck, she stroked the silky fabric. It was a long scarf. I had to wrap it around her neck several times. When I leaned closer, she cupped my chin with both hands. She asked, "Whatsa matter?"

"Nothing, Rose."

"Gracie." Her voice rose on the second syllable like a sitcom mom talking to her sitcom child.

"Must be the glasses. You've never seen me in glasses before."

"No. It's those ridges between your eyebrows like the ones you got when I used to make you eat broccoli."

I lowered my face, and her hands slipped upward, framing the sides of my cheeks.

"I was just wondering." I concentrated on wrapping the scarf loosely around my mother's neck. "I think this'll need a clip to hold it in place."

"Just wondering what?"

"About my dad," I said softly, and her shoulders stiffened. Still on my knees, I continued arranging the scarf. "Like, how do I know he was really my father? I don't look anything like the man in the photo."

"Gracie, look at me." She jerked my face up with a roughness I'd never felt from her before.

"Why don't I look like him?" I teared up.

"There are things you can't see in pictures. You have his hands, his shape fingernails."

"Why don't I look like him? I look more like Uncle Bernie and Uncle Mac."

"Grace, I'm too tired for this nonsense." She reached for the remote hanging from the bedrail, jammed her thumb down on the call button, and yelled into the speaker, "Nurse. I need you. Now!" She wouldn't meet my eyes. Her lips had disappeared into a tight line.

I hugged her. "I'm sorry. I didn't mean to hurt you." She'd become a rigid tree trunk. I stood up and backed away just as an aide rushed in. "What's wrong, Mrs. Giordano?"

"I want to be alone."

The aide turned to me. "Who are you?"

"Her daughter."

Her eyes widened, and she turned back to my mother. "Do you really want her to..."

"Yes. Please."

The aide looked at me again with raised shoulders and palms turned up in a what-should-I-do-here gesture.

I answered with a shrug.

I put on my jacket and bent to kiss my mother on the cheek. She was unresponsive. "Zoe and I will see you tomorrow night to celebrate your birthday," I said. Her expression softened ever so slightly at the mention of her granddaughter's name.

The next day, I left the office early and picked Zoe up at school so we could spend time alone with Rose before dinner. Zoe couldn't wait to give her grandmother the book she'd bought her about historic South Philadelphia. When she did so, Rose was delighted with the gift. I watched the two of them huddled together on the loveseat, twelve-year-old Zoe's dark brown curls bouncing as she laughed at some story her grandmother was telling. I caught my reflection in the mirror behind them, still surprised to see my face with glasses. Rose's friends always said the three of us looked so much alike, we could be the Giordano triplets. This was the first time I got what they were talking about. Not only did we have the same thick, dark hair, but also wide-spaced eyes and toothy smiles.

"Know how you can tell a true South Philly Italian from a fake?" asked Rose.

"No, Gram. How?"

"Real Italians put *gravy* on their pasta, not *sauce*. Hey, Gracie, come over here and join us."

She was acting as if the two of us hadn't had words the night before. I pulled a chair up next to the loveseat, and we looked at the pictures of the old neighborhood and listened to Rose's stories about how things used to be until Comma Lady appeared at the door, announcing dinner. Rose put on her new scarf and got behind her walker. En route to the dining room, I learned that Comma Lady's name was Belle and that she was the older sister of Rose's childhood best friend.

The dining room looked as it always did, a symphony in white—hair, tablecloths, uniforms, food—the whole scene punctuated by the clunking and scraping of walkers and wheelchairs. Zoe and I sat at a table with Rose, Belle, and Angie Moretti, who lived down the hall from Rose and was the only woman in the room who dared to wear her hair in anything but the short, old-lady cut. It extended down her back in a long, thick braid.

Zoe, who inherited her grandmother's extroverted personality, entertained us with a blow-by-blow account of the meal as we ate. "And Mrs. Moretti dips her spoon into a mountain of white. Turnips? Mashed potatoes? Stay tuned for the exciting conclusion." My daughter wanted to be either a sports announcer or a news broadcaster and took every opportunity to practice her skills. My father must have been an introvert, which would explain why I chose to be a computer programmer.

Mrs. Moretti's plate, with its mound of potatoes or turnips, reminded me of the scene in *Close Encounters* where Dustin Hoffman built a model of the Devil's Tower out of mashed potatoes, so I hummed the theme from the movie. Rose gave a belly laugh, and for a moment I felt as colorful as my mother. Zoe, not understanding the reference, shot me an oh-Mom look. Rose added her own commentary. "An overcooked string bean hung from her fork like a limp...er...string bean."

Once again the ladies laughed, I blushed, and Zoe muttered, "I don't see what's so funny, Grandma."

Rose had wanted her granddaughter to call her by her first name, but I'd drawn the line. Now I was afraid my mother would tell Zoe exactly what was so funny, as she would have told me at that age, but thankfully she let it go.

A member of the wait staff brought a small cake to the table. After Rose blew out the candles, Zoe suggested that we adjourn to her apartment to eat the cake. We agreed it was a good idea. Zoe, cake plate in hand, led the procession to the elevator, stopping when she got to the mural. She stepped back, squinted, and then asked, "Where are you, Mom?"

"What do you mean? I'm right here."

"I mean on the mural. Where's your picture on the mural?"

"Not there. This is a picture of South Philly before I was born."

"Who says? It's just a made-up picture. You told me the people here can add whatever they want."

"Those people live here, so it's their picture."

She put the cake down on the little table with the Magic Markers and crossed her arms. "Where does it say you have to live here to write on that wall?" She picked up a marker and held it out. "Draw something. Draw yourself."

I took the marker but shook my head. Zoe stood cross-armed and pursed-lipped—a look that said, "I'm not moving till you do." Stubborn, just like her grandmother.

Stepping closer to the mural, I zeroed in on the brick row house on the corner where my mother had lived before she'd moved to Porter Street. My father probably spent time in that house before he went off to Vietnam. I could draw his face in the window, but Zoe would ask questions, and Rose would get all angry, and...not worth the trouble. So, I drew a little girl on the front stoop. She was wearing a pink dress with white trim. It was my Easter dress. My favorite. I stepped away, then back, picked up a yellow marker, and drew a locket around her neck. I pulled a fine-tip ballpoint pen out of my hand bag and wrote, "To Gracie G. with love from Daddy" in letters so tiny, even someone with perfect vision would have to squint to read it.

Done. Now we could go upstairs and eat cake, and I could give Rose the snake bracelet. No more questions about my father. Time to forget the past.

But the past didn't forget me. A week after Rose's birthday, I came home from work to find Zoe sitting at the dining room table, matting and framing the elaborate family tree she'd made for her seventh-grade genealogy project. When Zoe had brought her report home the month before, I'd glanced at the family tree and then focused on the bright red A++ in the corner of the chart and the teacher's glowing comments on the written report: "Zoe is an excellent interviewer and a compelling writer. She could be a great investigative reporter someday." I'd been too busy to take a good look at her work and figured I'd get to it later. But Zoe had taken everything up to her room, and I forgot.

Now, as I looked at the picture, I realized something was off. "This is great, Zoe." I pointed to a name I'd never heard before. "But who's this?"

"That's grandpa's brother, George. You told me you knew the whole family history."

Brother? Rose had made a big deal about my father being an only child like her, like me, and now like Zoe. But there it was: two parallel lines descending from the horizontal that connected my paternal grandparents, Abigail and Roger Bishop, in holy matrimony. The first line was for George Bishop and the second for my father, Albert Bishop. My face was burning.

"Mom?"

"What? Oh, George. Of course I knew about him. Just forgot. What a dope," I said, tapping my forehead and turning away before she could see my red face. As Zoe went on describing her interviews with Rose and with her grandparents on my ex-husband's side, I wondered whether Rose had lied to Zoe or had been lying to me.

"Mom. You're not listening. I want to finish this and get to my homework. The report's in my room if you want to read it. Blue folder on my desk."

"Why don't you leave the family tree here when you're done framing it. It should hang downstairs where everyone can see it."

"Sure."

When Zoe went upstairs, I took her seat at the table and examined the family tree more carefully. The entry for George Bishop was dated 1942–1969. Albert Bishop's entry was dated 1944–1978. 1978? Rose told me my father died in 1972. If he was actually alive until 1978, when I was eight years old, I would have known him. But I had no memory of him. What was going on? My heart pounded. Maybe she'd gotten the dates wrong. I had to get my hands on that report to see if there were more clues.

I waited till Zoe was asleep and went upstairs to her room. The nightlight was on, and I could see her lying on her stomach, her default position. When she'd been an infant, my husband and I would lay her down on her back like the experts recommended, but within an hour we'd find her face down. After countless self-rearrangements, he and I decided to ignore the experts' warnings and let her be, realizing that parts of our daughter's life were already out of our control. Just like my marriage would be eight years later, when my husband started bringing me flowers and making unexpected moves in bed. I believed him when he told me he was trying to reignite our romance, even though he'd never been that kind of guy. Only after I overheard a phone call did I understand that he was an ex-husband-in-training. Our divorce followed soon after.

I picked up the folder and pulled out the stapled sheets. Zoe took a ragged breath, and I froze, but she resumed her normal breathing. Not that I was sneaking in—she'd said I could get the report from her desk—but I didn't want to get into a discussion. I took the report out into the hall, leaned against the banister, and read:

Interview with Rose Giordano. November 4.

Zoe: Did my grandpa have brothers and sisters?

Rose: Albert had a brother two years older than him who also went to Vietnam. His brother was killed in 1969 when his helicopter was shot down.

Zoe: Did you ever meet his brother?

Rose: No, but Albert talked about him all the time. He idolized his brother.

Wrong. My father was the one killed in Vietnam when he was shot down. I closed my eyes—the eyes that looked more like the "uncles' eyes" than my father's. *His brother.* Rose must have made it up. But why? To make our family history more interesting? It wasn't like her to lie. Maybe Rose had unwittingly told her the real story. Zoe could be persuasive and persistent. She already had a reporter's instinct, digging in when things didn't make sense to get at the truth.

There was one additional surprise in the report:

Zoe: How did Grandpa die?

Rose: Cancer. I couldn't be with him when he died, and it still makes me cry whenever I think about it.

I put the report back on her desk and looked at my daughter sleeping peacefully. I couldn't resist smoothing the hair at the back of her neck. My daughter was strong. Considering all she'd been through the last couple of years—her parents' messy divorce, her father's remarriage—she'd handled it amazingly well, probably better than I'd have at her age. When she'd heard her father was remarrying, she'd hung a "Shit Happens" poster in her room and offered to get one for me. I didn't want to encourage the use of profanity, but what the hell. I told her to get me one just like hers. Zoe's teacher was right. She'd make a great investigative reporter someday—or a great psychologist.

I sometimes wondered if Zoe's strength came from her having the one thing I'd never had: a flesh-and-blood father whose flesh might have been weak but whose love for his daughter was unconditional. At least I'd been able to give her that. And he'd given her something tangible, as well: a gold locket like the one that hung around my neck. I fingered my locket, the one that my alleged father had allegedly given me. Rose told me I used to put it in my mouth when I was little, but years of constant wear had smoothed out the teeth marks. The heart-shaped locket had nothing inside. No lock of hair. No trace of him.

Zoe knew where her locket had come from; she'd felt her father's fingers as he fastened the chain around her neck. My heart was empty. For all I knew, Rose could have ordered my necklace from some catalogue, a consolation prize for growing up fatherless. Had he ever seen me? Had he even known I existed? According to the dates on Zoe's chart, it appeared that my father had survived the war. Truth or fiction? I wouldn't know for sure till I questioned my mother.

I closed my eyes and was visited by a fragment of a memory. A man standing over my bed, whispering, *She's got your ears.* I remember asking Rose about it when I was four or five. She told me it was Santa Claus. I still believed back then.

My empty vessel of a heart was bursting with anger, and I wanted to drive to Oakwood and confront her. But how could I lash out at the woman who had sacrificed so much for me? What if I didn't like her answers? What if I got no answers?

I decided it was time to visit the storage locker where we'd parked most of Rose's possessions when she moved to assisted living. Who knew what else I would find among the tchotchkes? In the past, I'd riffled through some of the cartons to retrieve specific pieces Rose had requested, but this time I'd bring a flashlight and dig deep.

The next morning, I called in sick and drove out to the storage facility. Storage City, just north of Philadelphia, was a sprawling complex, large enough to qualify for its own zip code. I unlocked the metal entrance gate and drove the long path to Rose's storage unit. The doors of the drab gray buildings were color coded by sections in eye-popping shades, a juxtaposition at once funereal and festive. I parked in the lot for section P, located unit P55, inserted the key, and raised the purple metal grate, releasing a musty basement smell. When I switched on the lights, only two of the four lightbulbs worked, shedding just enough light for me to see where everything was. The boxes were unmarked, and I didn't know what I was looking for, but I promised myself I wouldn't leave until I'd fine-tooth combed every last carton and found something that would reveal the truth about my father. I'd forgotten to bring a box cutter, so I used a key to rip the first box open. It was filled with objects wrapped in newspaper, which turned out to be knickknacks. I pulled out a few to bring to my mother and put them in my tote.

On to the second carton. Dishes. I unwrapped a place setting of familiar melamine plates. The oversized orange and gold flowers looked garish, even in the dim light. The taste of spaghetti smothered in homemade gravy and topped with one of Rose's gigantic meatballs came to my tongue. I closed the carton and shoved it aside. This was *not* a stroll down memory lane; it was an investigation. And Rose already had enough dishes in her apartment to meet her needs.

The third box gave off a faint whiff of lavender when I opened it. Neatly folded dresses, skirts, and blouses spanning the styles of the fifties and early sixties revealed themselves to me. They were at least two sizes too small for present-day Rose. I pushed the box aside, impatient to find whatever it was I was looking for.

Inside the fourth carton was a jumble of old negligees and lace undergarments. Hidden beneath them was an old Strawbridge and Clothier hat box. I removed the top of the box and lifted out a mess of Playbills and cocktail napkins. Underneath was a stack of envelopes tied with a faded ribbon.

My hands shook as I picked up the letters. No way I could read them in the dim light, so I closed the locker and walked over to my car. Once inside, I untied the frayed ribbon. All the envelopes were written in the same hand, some bearing the address of our apartment on Porter Street and others of our house in Upper Darby, where we'd moved when I was ten. The envelopes were ordered chronologically, the earliest ones written in 1969 and the last one postmarked September 14, 1978. None of them had return addresses.

I read the first couple of letters, dropping them on my lap when I was finished. My body was stiff with tension. As I rubbed my shoulders and stretched my neck, I digested what I had read. I knew the identity of my father, and it wasn't Uncle Bernie or Uncle Max. I continued reading, and the story slowly unfolded—how they'd met, the circumstances of their relationship. The answers to all my questions. It took me an hour to read every word of those letters, from first to last. As I read, my numbness morphed into anger at her lies. I couldn't remember how many times she told me she'd never lie to me. My mother. My best friend, Rose. How completely I'd believed her, just like I'd believed in the Tooth Fairy and Santa Claus for way too long.

I put the letters back in their envelopes and retied them so I could hand them to Rose just as she'd left them. I was about to drive away when I remembered the damn knickknacks. I retrieved them from the locker and set off for Oakwood. I wanted to hear my mother admit to the truth.

Rose was sitting by the window reading a magazine when I walked in. "Gracie, I was just thinking about you," she said, her welcoming smile washing over me like warm spring rain, briefly cooling my anger. I put my tote bag down on the table next to her and told her I'd brought her knickknacks. "I'll help you put them on the shelf later," I said, "but first I have something to discuss with you."

I don't think she heard the emotion in my voice, because she got busy unwrapping the first knickknack, a porcelain geisha figurine someone had brought her from Japan. I took the packet of letters out of my purse and held them out to her. "Why didn't you tell me?" There was a sharp edge to my voice that both saddened and empowered me, and my mother looked up. It took a few seconds for recognition to register; then my mother slumped in her chair. Her "Oh" was little more than a sigh.

I dragged a chair in front of her and sat down, the stack of envelopes on my lap. When I tried to untie the ribbon, the frayed material ripped, and she grimaced as if I'd ripped something vital inside her. Her face was colorless.

"Why didn't you tell me my father was alive when I was a little girl?"

Rose straightened her back and raised her chin. "It was all such a long time ago. Why such a big deal all of a sudden? You're thirty-nine years old, Gracie, for God's sake. A big girl." At that moment she was the mother I remembered. The woman who was always in charge.

But I wasn't going to let her take charge of this. "When you don't have a father, it's *always* a big deal. *You* had a father. All I had was uncles."

"No. You had a father," she said, looking across the room at the photo, her eyes misting.

"Why did you lie to me?" My voice was as brittle as dried straw. "You knew how much I wanted...needed my father. Even when I stopped asking questions, you knew how much I missed him."

"How could I have known?" Her eyes narrowed in confusion.

"Because you read my diary."

Her face reddened.

"I knew you read it because sometimes it wasn't where I'd left it. And you're the only one who could have moved it. After a while, I locked it away. But still"—my eyes filled—"still I trusted you. You were my best friend. I called you Rose. No more... *Mother.*" I spat the word out like a curse, and she flinched.

"I know about Robert," I said. "I know about Ella, Pottstown, everything. The whole story is in these letters." I picked up the letters and waved them in my fist. Rose's eyes widened and her face melted in a sea of tears.

When my mother met Albert at a USO reception in 1969, he was married to Ella, a beautiful but sensitive girl prone to depression. When he and Ella had been dating, she'd made him promise he'd never leave her. It was a promise he kept. He was convinced she'd kill herself if he didn't, and then he'd be responsible for her death. It's not that he didn't love Ella, but he'd found the love of his life in Rose. Unfortunately, he'd met the two women in the wrong order. Then he went overseas, to Vietnam.

My father came home on leave at the end of 1970, shortly after I was born. He came home for good in 1971, leaving his only brother behind. He and Ella moved to Pottstown, a safe distance away from Philadelphia, but over the years my father scheduled frequent afternoon "meetings" and overnight "business trips," when he'd spend late-night hours at our house.

In some of the letters, he told my mother he wanted to wake me up and hug me and tell me who he was. But she insisted that what they were doing was a sin; if I knew his identity, she said, I might talk to my friends about him. The whole thing could become public, and the truth could end up killing his wife and destroying their lives.

"I trusted you," I said, my voice as hard and cold as granite, "but you didn't trust me. To keep a secret. Even though you knew what a good girl I was, always following the rules, always doing what you told me."

My mother was crying, but I tried not to let myself care. She wiped her eyes with the back of her sleeve as the tears kept coming.

"Every time I asked about him, you withdrew. I could see the pain in your face, and I respected it, *Mother*. I shut up." In some perverse way, I found myself gaining strength from my mother's vulnerability, and I hated myself for it. "You're the one who said *I* was too sensitive. I know I was, and all I wanted to be was strong like you. But now I know the score. *You* were the sensitive one."

"Stop it, Gracie. Listen to me. It was like the kind of love you see in the movies. Albert and me, we made you. I love you even more than I loved him. I love you more because both of us are there," she pointed to my heart, "inside you."

I rubbed the fourth finger of my left hand, the indentation that remained from my dead marriage. Even as I recognized the depth of my mother's emotions, I couldn't stop the anger that propelled my words.

I stood up, letting the envelopes that had been on my lap fall to the floor.

A knock at the door. A woman's voice. "You okay in there?"

I ignored her and barreled on. "I trusted you, Mother. You were all about honesty. 'Whatever you want to know, Gracie. Just ask. The birds and bees? No problem. Neighborhood gossip? Ask away. Anything.' Anything but the one thing I wanted to know. He wanted to wake me, but you said no. I can't—" I stormed out of the room, barely missing Belle, who was standing just outside the door, shaking her head.

Zoe was at a sleepover party, so the house was empty when I got home. I sat at the dining room table, took off my glasses, and lay my head down on my folded arms. My father had been right there in the next room with my mother, doing I don't want to think about what, while I slept. The two of them had come into my bedroom but had never awakened me. Not once, even though he'd wanted to. Had he put his hand on the back of my neck, smoothing my hair, the same way I smoothed Zoe's? He got to touch me, and all I got was flocked wallpaper. He hadn't mentioned children in the letters, but who knows? I could hunt them down and maybe find a whole new family with another little girl in a pretty pink dress like the one I wore that Easter.

I remembered that dress so well. A dress my mother could barely afford, but she knew how much I wanted it, so she probably worked overtime to buy it for me. I dropped a chocolate popsicle down the front of the dress the first time I wore it, and I was inconsolable. Rose had hesitated a split second before saying, "Gracie, those brown spots are just what that dress needed. It was so boring without it." I had loved my mother so much at that moment. As much as I loved Zoe.

Tomorrow, I would pick Zoe up from her friend's house, and we'd drive to Oakwood. Zoe and I would stop in front of the mural, and I'd draw brown spots on the little girl's pink dress. I'd tell her the story about the chocolate popsicle and how my mother's love had transformed a stained pink dress into something beautiful. Then we'd go to my mother's room and I'd beg her forgiveness for my outburst and tell her I understood why she'd kept my father's identity a secret—that by protecting his reputation, she'd also been protecting me. After all, that's what good mothers do.

Dot

If my name were Dot,
I'd have it embroidered in red letters
inside a red circle
on a white blouse,
and I'd work at a diner
somewhere far away,
like Idaho.

If my name were Dot,
I'd greet the regulars
and pour liquid happiness
into white cups with rounded lips.
Let me top that off, hon, I'd say,
because a good waitress
always *hons* her customers.

If my name were Dot,
I'd serve huge slices of homemade pie,
and the owner would scold me
because I didn't charge extra,
but I'd do it anyway

because pie is love.
Especially coconut custard.

If my name were Dot,
my parents would have all that money
they spent to send me to college
to become a psychologist,
and they'd be able to afford a condo in Florida
and go to early-bird specials
and play shuffleboard
and take a cruise to Fiji.

If my name were Dot,
I wouldn't need a Ph.D. in psychology
or a high-rent office,
and I wouldn't have to fight Blue Cross
or have an unlisted number.
I could serve meatloaf instead of prescribing meds
for the guy who lost his job.
And no one would sue.

If my name were Dot,
I wouldn't have to say, "Sorry our time is up,"
or read the DSM
to know what was bugging them,
and instead of seeing my own shrink twice a week,
I'd order up a toasted cinnamon bun
with lots of extra butter.
I wish my name were Dot.
But it's not.

The Black Button

Rachel Greenberg hunched over the sewing machine, feeding it endless yards of cloth. The beast was hungry, and she used little rewards to get herself through. *Three more seams and I'll wipe the sweat off my face. Just let me finish this shirt and I'll take a second to pin back my hair.* If she concentrated hard enough, she could block out the roar of the beasts and the rows of girls like herself churning out shirts and dresses none of them could afford, while the boss watched them from above like the Almighty surveying His creation. Steam shrouded the room, as if sitting *shiva* for the death of her childhood.

She drank as little water as possible to prevent "accidents," but sometimes her bladder betrayed her during the endless, heartless shifts, because they weren't allowed to get up.

Focus. Concentrate on the center of the universe—the spot where needle meets cloth. But her mind would wander. The blue of the fabric beneath her hands was almost the exact shade of her neighbor Sammy's eyes. From her apartment window, she would watch him play ball on his stoop, and she remembered the neighborhood call and response when the sun dipped behind the tenements.

"Schmuley, time for dinner."

"Who's Schmuley? This is America, Ma—call me Sammy."

"Smart mouth. Get in here before I give you such a *potch in tuchas* you won't sit for a week."

They were still neighbors, but Sammy was now eighteen, a few months older than her. With his red hair, blue eyes, and freckles, he looked so Irish his friends called him Sammy O'Goldberg.

Rachel cried out when the needle wandered off the edge of the cloth, nicking her index finger. If the boss had seen this error, her momentary loss of focus would cost her dearly; she'd have to pay to replace the blood-stained piece of cloth. Rachel looked up at the glass platform and saw fat Mr. Harris, pointing and gesturing for her to come up to his office.

She was momentarily paralyzed, remembering her last encounter with her boss three months earlier. She'd returned a few minutes late from her lunch break, and he'd intercepted her and led her up to his private office behind the glass platform. He'd slowly backed her into a corner, threatening to fire her, his jowly red face so close to hers she thought she'd choke on the rank cigar stink of his breath. Then he squeezed her breast so hard she gasped, but before she could cry out, he thrust his tongue in her mouth. Rachel tried to push back but was trapped by the weight of his bulk. She wanted to bite his tongue and scream, but no one would have heard her. He cupped her backside through the material of her skirt, drawing her even closer. Next, he would... Her heart hammered against her rib cage, and there was a pounding in her ears. No, not in her ears. At the door.

Mr. Harris released her. "Fix yourself up. You look like a whore."

She straightened her clothing and smoothed back her hair as he opened the door. A young male assistant looked at her, then at him, and then back at her and winked.

After the incident, rage and fear waged a civil war within her, sapping her energy and concentration. Sometimes she could barely restrain herself from screaming out in frustration and anger; but mostly she kept her head down in an attempt to make herself as invisible as possible, determined to tough it out until she could leave. To her relief, Mr. Harris failed to recognize her when their paths crossed, most likely because there were so many other girls to prey on—girls who disappeared regularly into his office. Those girls never spoke openly of what went on behind closed doors, but Rachel suspected he'd gone a lot further with some of them who, unlike her, had not been saved by a knock on the door. She couldn't imagine that any of them had gone willingly; she'd seen their fear-chiseled expressions when they were summoned, and the burning shame that colored their cheeks after their "private sessions." He robbed them of their self-respect along with their virtue.

Though Rachel never told her parents what had happened to her, she did begin a campaign to convince them she'd be more useful at home. Her father had recently started a business selling children's dresses that her mother and aunt sewed at home, and Rachel harangued him daily about joining them.

"No," said her father. "We'd have to buy a third sewing machine. Who's going to pay for that? And even if we could afford it, where would we put it?" He shrugged and held out his arms to encompass the parlor of the small two-bedroom apartment into which they'd managed to squeeze two sewing machines.

"When Mama and Aunt Jenny take breaks, I could take over and—"

He shook his head. "We've just started this business, Racheleh. We're depending on your salary to help make ends meet until we turn a profit."

Tears came to her eyes when he used the childhood diminutive of her name, reminding her of a time when she felt protected by her parents. But she was no longer a child. "I've been working at Harris and Sons since I was twelve," she said, "and I'm almost eighteen."

"We've all worked hard, Racheleh. Your brother and I walk the streets every day with our carts, rain or shine, selling odds and ends."

If only she could tell her father what Mr. Harris had done to his Racheleh, but who knew what a confession like that would do to him. "Why don't I show you how fast I can put a dress together?" she said instead. And that Sunday, while her mother was doing laundry, she was able to produce almost as much as her mother and aunt combined in the same amount of time. Her parents finally agreed to let her quit her job in a couple more months; they'd use that salary to help them purchase a third sewing machine.

And now, just two weeks before her last day at the sweatshop, Mr. Harris was summoning her to his lair. As she mounted the stairs to the glass platform, she braced herself for God knew what; but instead of dragging her into his office, Mr. Harris yelled at her, calling her a "stupid cow." He told her he'd be deducting the cost of the ruined cloth from her wages and promised to fire her if she made one more mistake. She almost wished he'd fire her then so she could put the wretched place behind her. But better to have two more weeks' salary than go home emptyhanded.

Finally, *the* day came: her last day at the sweatshop. Only one more hour until the closing whistle would announce the beginning of the rest of her life. She'd have to work just as hard at home as she did at the sweatshop, but there would be no more quotas to meet, no more paying to replace bloodstained cloth and broken needles, and no more lecherous boss stalking her from above.

As Rachel picked up her lunch pail that last day, she spotted a black button on the floor by her foot—a button that had somehow escaped being bound forever to a piece of cloth. She hazarded a quick glance at the glass platform and didn't see anyone watching, so with pounding heart she slipped the button into her lunch pail. It was still possible someone had seen what she'd done—one of Mr. Harris' henchmen on the floor, or a girl seeing an opportunity to tattle to management in exchange for special treatment—so she was on alert all afternoon, until the final bell.

As she passed through the sweatshop doors for the last time, she thought, *I'm like that button. I'm unattached. I'm free.* She walked home holding the button tightly in her fist, compressing all her sweatshop experiences into that little black disk, squeezing her memories into something tangible. When she got home that night, she put the button in the memory bag she'd fashioned from one of her father's old shirts, next to a few other remnants from her past: the faded print dress she'd worn when she arrived in America; a tattered rag doll; a misshapen ball given to her by a little boy on the ship, his arms outstretched as if offering her a bouquet. She had plans for that button. She'd use it on a blouse for the daughter she hoped to have. It would be a beautiful blouse, far too beautiful for a girl to wear in a tenement neighborhood. But once they moved to a better place, it would be the perfect gift.

Though the family's two-bedroom apartment was cramped, it seemed like heaven to Rachel, compared to the sweaty hell she'd endured for so many years. Rachel shared one bedroom with her aunt and her grandmother, and her parents slept in the other. The parlor adapted like a living organism to the needs of the moment. Sewing machines in the center of the room were pushed against the faded wallpaper of its walls at night to create a bedroom for her brother, who slept on the couch. When the family took in boarders to help pay the rent, couch cushions were placed on the floor to create a makeshift bed.

The only break in the hectic rhythms of their lives was on Friday nights, when the family gathered around the small dining room table and Rachel's mother lit Shabbat candles. Though Rachel's family was not observant—they resumed work on Saturdays, a day of rest for religious Jews—they never deviated from the Friday-night ritual of candle lighting and Shabbat dinner. Rachel cherished those moments when the sight of three generations of Greenberg women, their faces bathed in candle-light, connected her to her ancestors. The few small treasures they'd brought from the old country—a samovar, silver Kiddush cups, a few framed photographs, porcelain knickknacks—were housed in the small breakfront alongside the table.

Some of their immigrant neighbors dreamed of returning home once they'd earned enough to support the families they'd left behind, but Jewish families like Rachel's knew they could never go back. It was in America, they believed, where better times lay ahead, the ones they'd earn through hard work and sacrifice.

In time, Rachel saved enough money to purchase fabric for the blouse she'd imagined on her last day at the sweatshop. The material was silk, with gold and ivory stripes, and it shimmered in the light like mother-of-pearl. Whenever Rachel had a break from sewing, cooking, and laundry, she worked on her project, a Gibson Girl blouse with a high collar and a yoke that fastened down the back. After she'd designed the blouse, she didn't take long to complete it.

"A Gibson Girl blouse might not be the best," warned Rachel's mother. "I don't think it will be in style much longer. Maybe you should make something more modern. Aunt Frieda saw a copy of *Ladies Home Journal* and said the styles are getting looser."

Rachel lifted her feet from the treadle. "Mama, I don't think a woman's curves will ever go out of fashion. Anyway, I'm making this blouse for someone who hasn't even been born yet. My daughter will honor the past even as she moves into the future. I'll tell her the stories of how we came here, how hard we worked to make a better life, how lucky she is to be a Jew in America."

Rachel had purchased enough black buttons for all but the top buttonhole. When the time came, she sewed on the black button from the factory floor. She hung the blouse in the back of a closet.

Ada Horowitz had heard the story of the blouse many times, but she'd never seen it. Shortly after her fiancé proposed, her mother, Rachel Greenberg Horowitz, pulled a box down from her closet shelf and handed it to Ada. "A little gift for your engagement," she said.

Ada sensed her mother's anticipation as she opened the box. Inside was an old-fashioned blouse. "Is this the blouse you made?" she said, trying to hide her disappointment.

Her mother nodded. Ada held the glimmering fabric up to the light; she tried to focus on its beauty and significance, not on the style.

"Oh, Mom," she said after a moment of hesitation, hoping her voice conveyed enough gratitude. She was touched by the gift, but she knew it was her mother's unspoken expectation that she would wear it on some special occasion, and Ada couldn't imagine an occasion where the blouse wouldn't be out of place. She was a modern woman, attuned to the fashions of the early 1940s. And as one of only two women in the freshman class at Temple University's law school, she had to be especially careful to dress in a way that didn't call attention to herself. This wasn't the first time she and her mother had clashed, sometimes subtly, sometimes overtly, about where Ada saw herself in a changing world.

"Let me try it on," said Ada, starting to unbutton the row of buttons down the back of the blouse. But her mother could read her emotions.

"Now that I see the blouse in the light," said Rachel, "after all these years, I can tell it's not your style."

"That's not—"

"It's all right, Adeleh. I know you appreciate the blouse, but it will sit in your closet. And that's okay." Rachel smiled and held out her hand to take back the blouse. "I'll just put it away for now."

That was her mother in a nutshell. Knowing just how to soothe hurt feelings and smooth awkward situations, a skill Ada worked hard to cultivate. Still, the use of the Yiddish diminutive of her name embarrassed her. Sometimes her mother acted so old world, so...Jewish.

"Thank you, Mom," she said, embracing her mother, inhaling the familiar lavender scent that had comforted her when she was a child, before she was aware of her mother's otherness. Not that Ada was ashamed of her history—or was she? Engaged to Kevin Carlson, a gentile, she found herself spending more time at the homes of her gentile friends than they spent in hers. She was reluctant to bring them to her Jewish Overbrook Park neighborhood and to introduce them to the mother with the Russian accent who threw Yiddish words into her conversation like matzo balls.

As she let her mother take the shirt from her hands, Ada resolved to show more appreciation for her mother and all she'd done. Rachel had started her own dressmaking business after her husband had died six years earlier, and she'd encouraged Ada to go to law school at a time when it was rare for women to choose that path. Ada and Kevin planned to live with Rachel until they both finished law school. Then they planned to move to the suburbs, across City Line Avenue—just blocks from Rachel's Overbrook Park row house, but a world away. They'd buy a colonial, maybe even a ranch, and fill it with sleek, contemporary furniture. Just thinking about this made Ada feel more American.

In her suburban ranch house, Ada polished the silver candlestick holders, removing the tarnish between the twists and turns of the stems, and then put them away. They'd been a house gift from Rachel, who said she wanted Ada to have them because they came from the old country. The candles had rested undisturbed in the curio cabinet until Ava's four-year-old, Sara, rushed into the kitchen after a morning at Sunday School.

"Why don't we do Jewish things? Why don't we make challah or light candles on Friday night?"

Kevin was the one who'd suggested their daughter get some religious education. Raised in the Congregational Church, he'd parted ways with organized religion in his teens, finding the whole thing meaningless; but when he met Ada, he discovered a lot he admired in Judaism: its focus on life on earth rather than the afterlife, its emphasis on knowledge and learning and questioning. His six-foot frame, blond hair, and blue eyes screamed *gentile*, but after he'd brought Sara to Sunday School a dozen times, he joked, "Sometimes I feel more Jewish than you." Ada laughed, but the comment stung.

So, at her daughter's request, on Friday nights, Ada began lighting candles in her ancestors' candlesticks. The first time she'd covered her head, waved her hand over the flames, and recited the blessing, she felt like the caricature of a Jewish bubba. Maybe if she continued to practice the ritual, she thought, it would feel more natural. Her daughter's happy face and wonder at the Hebrew words made her feel something—not quite religiousness, but at least a tiny sense of wonder. So, she kept at it, adding in the blessings over the wine and bread, which Sara chanted along with her. But even after several weeks, the gestures continued to feel awkward, the words empty. She stopped. Kevin encouraged her to keep trying, but she told him, "You know how you feel about going to church? That's how I feel about all this." He stopped trying to persuade her.

Sara was disappointed that they no longer lit the candles. Ada felt guilty and selfish. So, she made a concession to tradition by serving challah every Friday night and letting Sara lead the blessing.

Rachel converted her basement to a dress shop after Ada and Kevin moved out. She managed to squeeze a lot of clothing racks into a limited space, and the neighborhood ladies had no trouble finding what they were looking for. They went into the powder room to try things on.

And, of course, Sara loved to play among the dresses. Until recently, both Ada and Rachel had supervised her as she tried on the oversized dresses and twirled like a dervish in front of the three-way mirror. But as Sara got older, she dropped hints that she wanted to spend dress-shop time alone with her grandmother. So, Ada remained upstairs during these visits, catching up on paperwork for her legal cases, while her mother spent time alone with Sara.

On this particular day, Ada was having a hard time concentrating, as the sound of Sara's laughter kept drifting up the stairs. She put down her pen and tried to guess what the two of them were doing, unable to suppress a twinge of envy. She reminded herself that it was good for a child to have a close relationship with a grandparent. And yet...there it was, the flicker of jealousy over the fun her daughter was having with Rachel. Ada knew her mother was disappointed that she'd married a gentile, though Rachel had kept those feeling to herself. And she knew that the further she moved into the upscale Main Line suburbs and the friendlier she got with her mostly Christian neighbors, the greater the distance became between herself and her roots.

Ada opened the basement door a crack and yelled, "Five more minutes." She could have gone downstairs to speed things up but decided to let Sara spend the remaining time alone with her grandmother.

Eight-year-old Sara ducked under the racks, pretending she was lost in the jungle. Then she picked out a strapless gown with a beaded top and put it on. Holding up the long skirt, she stepped into a pair of high-heeled shoes from the collection her grandmother had scattered about for the ladies to wear when they tried on the clothes and began clunking around. Grandma Rachel sang, "Here she comes, Miss America," which made Sara laugh, because the Russian accent made it sound like, "Here she kumps."

When her mother yelled "Five more minutes" from upstairs, Sara was tempted to negotiate up to ten, but she knew she wouldn't succeed. As her grandmother helped her change back into her shorts and T-shirt, she wondered if her mother had ever played with the dresses when she was growing up. Then she remembered her mom telling her there hadn't been a dress shop back then. Even if there had been, Sara couldn't imagine her mother running around and playing dress-up like she did.

Rachel walked up the front steps of her daughter's split level with the huge front yard on the first night of Hanukkah. A new menorah stood in the window, and she smiled. Ada's new menorah was larger and more modern than her old one; this one had a long silver branch for the *shamas* candle rising at an angle from the base, with eight shorter branches angled off the long one for the rest of the candles. Not her taste, but her daughter's, which was as it should be. That's what we do, she thought. We take our old-world ways and weave them into the new. At four o'clock it was almost dark, and soon the menorah would be invisible until the candles were lit. A small miracle.

Rachel rang the bell and peered through the frosted glass door panel until Ada opened the door. When Rachel stepped inside, she was enveloped by the warmth of the room. It wasn't until she'd taken off her coat and handed Ada her shopping bag full of Hanukkah gifts that she saw the Christmas tree in a corner of the room. "Oy," she said softly, a chill coming over her.

Ada took a deep breath and searched for a reply. "It's blue and white, Mom. A Hanukkah bush."

Rachel pinched her lips and said nothing.

The two of them sat down on the sofa. The room was silent except for the ticking of the baseboard heaters. Then a door slammed, and ten-year-old Sara walked into the living room, arms laden with school books. "Sorry I'm late. The play rehearsal ran over and...Grandma, you're here!" She put her books down on a table and hurried over to her grandmother. "You okay?"

"Kevin grew up with a tree," said Ada, continuing the one-way conversation with her mother, "and I didn't want Sara to feel left out."

Sara took her grandmother's hand. "I don't feel left out."

"I'm sorry, Mom," said Ada. "I'll take the tree down if you'd like me to."

"That's for you and your husband to decide, Ada."

"I'll...we'll decide."

Ada set her mother's bag of gifts down on a table near the menorah. It was hard enough fitting in with her Christian neighbors and her colleagues at the law firm, where she was the only Jew. She wanted to reassure her mother that she was still Jewish on the inside, even if she didn't look or act like one. That this was nothing more than optics. But in her heart of hearts, Ada had to admit that she didn't really feel Jewish on the inside, which is how she explained to Kevin why she didn't want to light candles—that it didn't feel real to her. She regarded it as a compliment when people didn't recognize her as Jewish; and she was pretty sure no one knew at the law firm, where she wore her Gentile married name like a cloak of acceptability.

Ada looked at her mother and Sara standing hand in hand in front of the menorah in the window. It had been naïve to think her mother would accept the tree because they still celebrated Hanukkah as their main holiday. Christmas trees were not something she or her mother had grown up with, but there was nothing inherently Christian about an evergreen with a few bulbs on it, was there? In fact, Christmas trees felt more American to her than Christian.

Kevin's car pulled into the driveway.

"Dad's home," she said. "Sara, would you like to light the candles before we have dinner?"

Sara nodded forcefully. "And we'll all say the prayers."

Sara opened the door to her grandmother's row house and stepped inside. She was enveloped by the intoxicating smell of freshly baked brownies.

"Saraleh." Grandma Rachel hugged her. "Wonderful to see you." Sara loved how her grandmother pronounced "wonderful" as "vonderful," and the way she used the Yiddish diminutive of Sara's name, though she was almost seventeen. She especially loved the look of joy on her grandmother's face every time she opened the door, as if each visit were the first.

Sara stomped the snow off her boots and left them on the doormat. "Sorry I haven't been to see you in such a long time, but I've been studying for my PSATs, and rehearsing for the school show, and..."

"*Shah.* Come in. Get warm."

Grandma Rachel's house hadn't changed much since Sara's earliest visits. There was the old-fashioned treadle sewing machine, the gate-legged table from the family's first apartment in America, the samovar from the old country, and various and sundry tchotchkes, including the silver cup Grandpa Sam had won at a cakewalk dance contest in Atlantic City. When Sara had asked Grandma Rachel why the first prize in a cakewalk contest wasn't cake, her grandmother's tinkling laugh filled the room like a shower of silver coins.

She and her grandmother had planned to spend the afternoon knitting. Sara was looking forward to hearing her grandmother's stories. She'd probably heard all of them by now, but they never grew old in the retelling. Also, Grandma Rachel had promised Sara a surprise.

Sara sat down next to her grandmother on the couch and set her knitting bag beside her. She was knitting a sweater for her mother. "Can we do the surprise first?" she asked. A rhetorical question, since Sara knew her grandmother always saved surprises for last. Grandma Rachel's answer was a smile.

They knit together in silence, needles clicking. Sara added two inches to the front of the sweater before taking a brownie break, helping herself to one of the chocolate squares that were piled high on a floral china plate on the coffee table.

Rachel put down her needles and followed Sara's lead. "You thought you'd never learn to knit as fast as me and look at you." Rachel had taught Sara to knit European style when she was thirteen or fourteen. "You can go so much faster when you put the ball of yarn on the left side, Saraleh," she'd explained. "Just wrap it around your left index finger and make the stitches with your needle. Like this."

It had taken Sara a little while to get the hang of it, but Grandma Rachel had assured her that if she worked at it, Sara would get her own needles to fly as fast as hers.

Sara finished her last brownie and took up her knitting needles.

"See, Saraleh," said her grandmother. "Sometimes the old ways are better."

Sara nodded, suspecting that Grandma Rachel was making an oblique reference to her mother's embarrassment at what she considered the "old ways." Sara's family had joined a synagogue, but more often than not, Sara had to persuade her mother to take her to services. She wanted to ask her what was so hard about letting a little bit of the past seep into the present, but something stopped her. Maybe the two of them could have that conversation when she was older. But whenever Sara thought about her mother's reluctance to lean back into tradition, she felt sorry for her grandmother. And, in a way, for her mother.

Sara's visits to her grandmother's home were journeys into a sepia-toned past. Each story her grandmother told added a stroke of color.

"Tell me about the sweatshop, Grandma."

"You've heard that story a thousand times. You could probably tell it better than me."

"Maybe I could tell it, but you lived it."

"Oy, *mameleh*, I lived it." Grandma Rachel launched into the familiar story: the din of the machines, the oppressive heat, the owners intentionally blocking the exits so the girls couldn't take unauthorized breaks.

"In my history class, we just read about the Triangle Shirtwaist Company fire in New York," said Sara. "A hundred forty-five girls—mostly Jewish and Irish teenagers—burned, suffocated, or jumped to their death because they couldn't get out. Everyone thought sweatshops had only been in New York, but I told them it was the same in Philadelphia." Sara shuddered to think how easily Grandma Rachel's name could have been among the names in the obituary column.

Needles clicked in silence.

"Grandma, how did you keep your mouth shut in that terrible place?"

"Sometimes you have to keep your words inside so you don't lose your job...so you keep the peace."

"I can't imagine me or any of my friends working under conditions like that. Last spring, when the air conditioning wasn't working at school, the students complained so much that a bunch of parents threatened to take their children out of school until the system was fixed."

"Hothouse flowers, your generation," she said, letting out a puff of air. "One smack on the *tuchas* when they're young, and they spend the rest of their lives *kvetching* to some psychiatrist about their miserable childhoods."

Sara laughed. Had everyone back then been as strong as her grandmother? Was their strength born of necessity, genetics, or some combination?

"Time for the surprise," said her grandmother. The two of them put aside their knitting and walked upstairs to Rachel's bedroom. Her grandmother took a Strawbridge's box out of the closet and held it out. "This is for you."

Sara had no idea what to expect. With anticipation, she opened the box and pulled back the tissue paper. Lying there was the most beautiful blouse she'd ever seen. She put down the box and held up the blouse. It was like something from an old movie about high society in the Gilded Age. "Grandma, it's so beautiful," she gasped.

"Try it on."

"I'm afraid I'll mess it up. It's so delicate."

"I made it a long time ago, and it's been waiting to be worn ever since. Here, give it to me and I'll undo those buttons. See, they go all the way down the back." Her old fingers moved quickly over the row of black buttons. "Now take off your sweater," she told Sara. Sara complied, and Rachel helped Sara slip her arms into the sleeves. "Now turn around and I'll button the whole thing back up," Rachel said.

Sara was afraid the blouse would be too tight. Didn't those Victorian ladies wear corsets? She held her breath as her grandmother buttoned the blouse.

"It fits perfectly, as if it was made for you," Rachel said, her voice wistful. In front of Rachel's dresser, Sara stood on her toes, trying to see what she looked like in the dress.

"I wish you still had that three-way mirror from the dress shop, Grandma."

"Actually, I do." Rachel chuckled and took Sara's hand, leading her across the hall to the spare bedroom. She opened the closet door, and there it was. The two of them laughed as Sara twirled in front of the three-way mirror, feeling like a Victorian princess.

"Now, let me unbutton you," said Rachel tenderly. "Then we'll go downstairs and finish the brownies, and I'll tell you a new story."

Sara put her sweater back on as Rachel picked up the blouse and the box. Once they were seated on the couch again, Rachel handed Sara the blouse. "Look at the buttons on the back and see if anything stands out," she said.

It took Sara a moment to notice. "The top button is a little darker and smaller than the others," she said.

"Very good, Saraleh," said Rachel, patting Sara's arm. "Now I'm going to tell you the story of that button."

Her grandmother told her how she'd picked up the button on her last day at the sweatshop, how it represented both the strife of the past and the freedom that lay ahead. Sara began to cry. And to Sara's surprise, her grandmother, who had always kept her emotions in check, cried a bit, too.

Before Sara left, she gave her grandmother one last hug. Rachel's skin was as gossamer soft and silky as the blouse.

When I wear that blouse, Sara thought, I'll be wearing her memories. She lifted the box with the blouse. "I'll save this for a special, special occasion," she said.

"It's been waiting a long time for a special occasion," said Rachel. She kissed Sara on the forehead before closing the door.

Rachel told Ada she didn't want a fuss made over her eightieth birthday. So, Ada planned a small surprise: a gathering of family and friends at a cozy restaurant in Ada's neighborhood. Of course, the occasion demanded photographs on poster board, so Ada needed old photographs. She paid a secret visit to Rachel's house while her mother was out shopping with Sara.

Standing in Rachel's living room—*her* old living room— she was tempted to take her parents' wedding picture, which was hanging on the wall behind the samovar. But her mother would notice it was missing. Maybe her mother had a duplicate in the piles of photographs she'd never found the time to organize.

The wedding photograph had fascinated Ada when she was a little girl. She couldn't get over how young her parents looked. Her mother, a tiny slip of a woman with a round face, dark eyes, and delicate features, rested her arm on the shoulder of her father, who was seated next to her. Sam was fair-haired, handsome, and had a modern look about him, like someone out of a high-school yearbook. Rachel wore a long-sleeved, high-necked, white wedding dress, and her hair was dark and abundant, piled high in the fashion of the day. Ada and Sara had inherited Rachel's thick, dark hair, but Sara's eyes were blue, her nose was narrower, and her mouth was wider than Ada's and Rachel's.

Ada wondered if her mother still kept the old black photo album in the drawer under the coffee table. She opened the drawer, and there it was—an album with a cover so worn that it shed black cardboard chips when Ada opened it. Ada picked it up and sat down on the sofa like she'd done with her mother so many years ago. There was the faded photo of her father with his cousins at the beach, bunched together, wearing long jerseys over knee pants. When she was little, Ada imagined them racing each other to the ocean as soon as the photographer turned his back. On the next page was a group portrait that must have been taken shortly after the family had arrived in America. Her grandmother was sitting ramrod straight in the center of the photo, staring sternly at the camera, her hands on the lap of her long, dark skirt. Her father and uncle flanked the matriarch like bookends, dressed in identical double-breasted jackets that were a little too small. And there was her ten-year-old mother. Ada detected the hint of smile on her face, though she knew people back then weren't supposed to smile for photographs. Rachel wore a frilly white dress and white shoes, standing slightly pigeon-toed next to her brother, who had his arm on her shoulder. They were all so...alive.

One edge of the photo came loose from the hinge securing it to the page, and Ada gently slid it back into place. She remembered her mother telling her how lucky she was to have a visual record of her ancestors. Not to mention how lucky she was that her parents had left Russia when they did.

When Ada was in middle school, a Holocaust survivor had talked to her class about being the only one of her family to survive the camps. She told them how much she grieved—not only over the loss of her family, but also over her children's lost grandparents, aunts, and uncles. It was as if they'd never existed.

"When I die," Rachel had told her so many years ago, "these pictures will keep all of us alive for you."

Ada felt a heaviness in her chest.

Sara had told Ada she was planning to wear the blouse to her grandmother's birthday party as a surprise. But as Rachel used to say, "*Mann Tracht, Un Gott Lacht.*" Man plans, and God laughs. Rachel died one week short of her eightieth birthday. Instead of wearing the blouse at the Cozy Cottage Restaurant, Sara wore it at Montefiore Cemetery.

The mourners sat in folding chairs facing the open grave. A green canopy sheltered them from the sun. It was a small group: Ada and Kevin and Sara, some of their friends, Rachel's older brother, a few of Rachel's remaining friends. One by one, each member of the family stood and said a few words. Except Ada. She wanted to speak; as a lawyer, she'd never been at a loss for words. But on that day, she was mute. Not due to a loss of words, but because she had too many. So, she let Sara speak for her.

"Grandma Rachel once told me that she remembered her own grandmother," Sara began, "and that I'd probably live to see my own grandchildren. 'So right now, Saraleh,' she said, 'we share two hundred years of history between us.' As I looked into her eyes, it was like looking through a telescope into the past. I could almost see my great-grandparents, my great-great grandparents, and an unbroken line of all who came before. And I knew Grandma Rachel was looking into the future through my eyes."

As her daughter spoke, a ray of sunlight kissed the silky softness of her blouse. Ada thought, *How could I not have seen the beauty and love in my mother's creation? How could I have refused that gift?*

When Sara returned to her seat, Ada wrapped her arms around her daughter and didn't let go until the rabbi asked everyone to stand. Then they all chanted the traditional prayer, thanking God for the gift of memory.

Me Two

Helena hadn't been anywhere near the Mütter Museum in years, but now that her OB-GYN had moved into a classic nineteenth-century row home across the street, there was no avoiding it. As she descended the marble steps of the doctor's brownstone, the baby kicked with the five perfectly formed toes she'd seen in that day's sonogram. The kick seemed like a warning from the daughter inside her that she shouldn't revisit the dark period that the Mütter Museum brought to mind. The imposing entrance was just as she remembered—its wrought iron gate and Doric columns belying the grotesque medical oddities that lay within. The past had a stubborn way of insinuating itself into the present.

She'd been seventeen the day it all began, stopping off at her locker to pick up her artwork, nervous about her first one-on-one critique with her art teacher. She'd hesitated outside the art studio before knocking softly at the door.

"Right on time. Come in." Mr. Fletcher sat at his desk at the far end of the empty room. He waved her over. With his long hair and wire-rimmed glasses, he looked like a throwback to the sixties—only he was colorless, as if he'd missed out on all the fun.

Helena loved the art studio, with its olfactory stew of clay, glue, turpentine, acrylic, and oils, its walls plastered with student projects, its stained work tables. When the studio was bustling with students, it felt like home. But not today, when her first quarter's work was about to be judged. Clutching her stretched canvas and faux-leather portfolio to her chest, she slouched as she crossed the room to Fletcher's desk. Slouching was a bad habit but a comfortable one. She smiled nervously as she placed her work on his desk.

Fletcher acknowledged her with a half-smile; then he picked up the top canvas and held it up to the window. He ran a finger over the greens and browns of the primeval forest she'd painted, lingering on an indistinct figure near the edge of the canvas.

"Is this a place you've seen?" His face was impassive, withholding of judgment.

"No." Was that the right answer? Do real artists paint what's there or what isn't?

"Reminds me a little of Rousseau. Ever heard of him?"

"Uh-uh." Her voice was flat. Was that a compliment or a put-down?

"He paints wild forests with magical creatures lurking in the shadows. You should check him out at the art museum."

"Okay. I...I'll check him out." Helena didn't normally stutter, but she still had no idea what he thought of her work. She needed a good recommendation for her art school application. She shifted her weight from leg to leg.

"Why don't you sit down? Pull up a chair." He pointed to a stool at the closest work table.

She seated herself across from him, heart pounding, as he placed her canvas on an easel next to his desk and paged through her portfolio.

"Most of your landscapes are good. Excellent, actually."

Did he mean that? Through the years, other art teachers had told her she had promise, but she'd assumed they said that to every half-decent art student.

Fletcher looked up from her work and met her gaze before she could turn away. She thought she detected "the look," a subtle—sometimes not so subtle—signal that a guy had designs on her body. Usually, he'd then give her the up-and-down before making his next move. After fending off too many guys who had touched her body as if it was theirs to possess, she'd sworn off dating until she found someone who could see *her*. But now Fletcher's face was all business, so she must have been mistaken.

The bell rang, signaling the end of last period, but Helena wasn't ready to leave.

"So, you really think my work is good?"

"I do." He slipped a drawing out of its plastic sleeve and stood it on the easel in front of the canvas. "I'm especially impressed by these—I'm not sure what to call them—imaginative worlds. Some of your figures are quirky, comical. I like this one, too," he said, pulling out another drawing: a Humpty Dumpty-shaped man wielding a conductor's baton and tossing a musical score into the air. "But the most interesting ones to me are these." He took out two more sketches and put them side by side on the easel. "The elongated forms that look like they've been extruded. The missing limbs, this is the stuff of nightmares. They're so different from your other work. There's something dark and disturbing about them, qualities that make your work unique."

She'd just been messing around, not thinking of anything dark. But perhaps he was helping her discover her artistic voice.

"Something about them reminds me of the Mütter Museum," he continued. "Ever heard of it?"

Helena shook her head.

"It's a medical museum. Been around since the 1800s. Specializes in anatomical specimens, medical anomalies, bizarre surgical instruments. It's a little creepy, but—"

There was a knock at the door. "Sorry to interrupt," came a voice Helena recognized as her sister's. "Just need to tell Helena something. I'll be quick."

"Okay," said Fletcher, a frown clouding his face.

Her sister opened the door and stood on the threshold. She was short, slightly overweight, with frizzy brown hair. "Hey, Lena. Just wanted to let you know I'll be waiting for you outside the main entrance."

"Thanks, Jen," said Helena. "I'm almost done."

"Who was that?" asked Fletcher when the girl had left.

"My sister."

"You don't look at all alike. Is she older, younger?"

"Same age. We're twins."

"Twins?" His eyes widened. "Hard to believe."

Yes, it was hard for most people to believe. Unlike her sister, Helena was tall, with almond-shaped eyes and straight black hair that someone once described as an Oriental silk curtain. She didn't look like someone who could have shared a womb with Jenna.

"There's a pair of twins at the Mütter. Siamese—no, they call them 'conjoined' now. You can't miss them." Fletcher handed Helena the sketches, canvas, and portfolio. He's such a nerd, she thought as she slipped the sketches back into their plastic sleeves. Maybe even gay. She was sure she'd been mistaken about "the look."

"I'd like to help you find your artistic voice," he said. "Are you ready to be pushed?" His expression was earnest.

Yes, it's about time someone pushed me. She was afraid he might get the wrong idea if she said that aloud, so she just nodded.

"I'd like to meet with you once a week. Will that work for you?"

She nodded.

"Let's say Wednesdays, last period. Looks like neither of us have classes then."

Helena thanked him and left the room. She stood outside the closed door for a moment to gather her thoughts. She felt lighthearted, lightheaded, almost giddy. She'd been drunk one time, and that's how she felt. Drunk on his praise.

Helena met her sister outside, and they walked the half mile home as they did most days, weather permitting. The elms and chestnuts on the street were still holding onto the last of their yellow leaves, the maples clutching a few red ones; most had browned and dropped. The girls' footsteps echoed with the crunching sound of late October.

"What happened in there?" asked Jenna. "You're glowing. Did he—"

"Oh, Jen, you wouldn't believe it. He thinks I'm a good artist. Really good."

"Of course, your work is good. Can't understand why you don't believe it when people tell you you're good at something."

Because most of the compliments I receive are powered by ulterior motives.

They turned the corner onto their street. "Fletcher told me I should visit the Mütter Museum for inspiration."

"Whoa," said Jenna, putting her hand on Helena's shoulder and turning to face her. "That's totally creepy."

"He admitted it was a little creepy but—"

"I've read about that place, seen photos. All those bits and pieces of human anatomy gone wrong." Jenna's brow was furrowed. "Hey, it makes sense *I'd* be interested in the Mütter since I'm going to med school, but why you?"

"He told me there was something about my work that reminded him of the Mütter. But why recommend that museum and not the work of, say, Hieronymus Bosch or Escher?"

"Beats me."

"How's about we go together next Saturday? I'll bring my sketchpad, and you bring your notepad."

Helena and Jenna stepped wide-eyed into the exhibition hall, its walls lined with dark wooden display cases. "So weird. So retro," said Helena. "All those wood cabinets and cases and that old oak smell."

They walked up and down the aisles, gawking at the cases

crammed full of medical oddities: skulls, organs in jars, amputated limbs. What was he thinking when he sent me here? she thought. *This* is what he saw in my drawings? This is a freak show. She concluded that he'd been making fun of her work but that she'd misinterpreted his words as praise.

Jenna paused in front of an object that resembled a giant stuffed worm. "Freaky," she said, reading the label. "This guy had a forty-pound colon. They called him the Human Windbag. Fletcher thought this would inspire you?"

"Yeah. I was just thinking the same thing. Guess he's full of shit." Helena was trying for levity, but Jenna gave her a quizzical look. Some of her anger at Fletcher must have seeped into her voice. Best to forget about Fletcher and enjoy an afternoon with her sister.

They continued their exploration, softly calling out to each other when they found something especially mindboggling. Helena came across a cabinet filled with objects that people had swallowed. "You've got to see this, Jen." She read the labels on the drawers: "Pins, hardware, bones, nuts, false teeth. Some doctor removed all this stuff." This museum was clearly her sister's bailiwick.

They stopped at the Soap Lady, a figure in a case stretched out like a mummy, her mouth a gaping hole. Some chemical reaction had changed her skin to wax. The sign read: *Remarkably, the body maintains both its overall shape and appearance.* "Hey, Jen. Chemistry. Isn't that your thing?" But her sister had moved on to a case of wax models showing the ravages of rare skin diseases.

"Right up Dad's alley," said Jenna. "Do you think he came here when he was a med student?" She took a notebook and pen out of her bag. Leaning in to read the description under some human part that had gone awry, she began to write.

Up ahead Helena spotted the plaster casts of the twins. She wondered if that's why Fletcher thought she'd be interested in the Mütter. But he'd suggested the place before he'd known she was a twin. She walked over to the life-sized plaster torsos. The twins stood face to face, an arm over each other's shoulder. She read the yellowed label:

Chang and Eng were conjoined twins. This plaster cast was made from their bodies after their autopsy was performed at the Mütter. Their conjoined livers are displayed on the shelf below. They were the original "Siamese Twins," though they were actually three-quarters Chinese. After spending much of their lives on exhibition, they married sisters and settled as farmers. Chang was a heavy drinker with a bad temper, while Eng was placid and easygoing.

Had they fought, she wondered. Had they tried pulling apart? Was one smarter than the other? Handsomer? *Jen and I are so different yet so close. How would it feel to wear my sibling like an appendage?*

Helena sat down on the floor, took a black pastel out of her purse, and sketched a rough outline of the twins. She drew a beer mug in Chang's hand but found the image cartoonish and ripped it out. She redrew the two brothers, focusing on the point of junction between the two.

Helena drew them in endless variations—joined at the stomach, hips, chest. She drew her face on one twin, her sister's on the other. She turned to a fresh page and drew the two of them with their heads conjoined. *If we shared a brain, we'd have equal value in our parents' eyes.* Jenna was a math genius born into a family of scientists, and Helena was an artist—something that couldn't be measured in IQ points—a talent as welcome as weeds in a rose garden. Once she dreamed she heard her mother telling Jenna, "Nine months smack up against each other. Couldn't you teach your sister something useful?"

Helena abandoned drawing after drawing, trying to capture something elusive on paper, something she was feeling but not seeing.

Jenna tapped her on the shoulder, and she jumped.

"Lena, my brain is fried. You wanna go?"

"I'm not ready yet. Why don't you go and we'll catch up later?"

"Okay. I can see you're really into it. Take your time."

Helena watched her sister leave, remembering the two of them when they were eleven or twelve, standing back to back before a mirror, comparing heights. Jenna had said, "You're so lucky, Lena."

She'd answered, "Me?"

"Yeah. 'Cause you're so pretty."

She remembered her answer. "Are you kidding? You'll always be ten minutes older and three grades smarter than me, Jenna. That makes you the lucky one in the family."

Their parents had tried to treat them the same. But Jenna was a mirror reflecting their parents' ordinary features and extraordinary gifts. Their mother was a tenured physics professor at Penn, their father a world-renowned dermatologic oncologist. Don't all parents favor their mirror-image children? Her parents had seemed to smile with their whole faces when they looked at Jenna's papers covered with stars and smiley faces.

Helena left the museum an hour later. On the bus home, an older man sat down next to her, though there were plenty of empty seats. She clutched her sketchbook to her chest and turned to the window, but she couldn't avoid his reflection and the eyes that undressed her. When guys said they wanted to go out with her because she was "nice," their eyes told her a different story. Her only male friend was Elliot, who was gay and whose mouth and eyes told the same story. When Mr. Fletcher had slipped her drawings out of their plastic sleeves, he, too, had smiled with his whole face.

Helena and Fletcher met weekly, mostly in the studio but occasionally in his office when the studio was in use. During their first few meetings, she was nervous as she spread her compositions out on his desk in the studio, heart pounding as he took notes with his green pen and critiqued her work. His criticisms stung at first, but she gradually realized he was challenging her to grow as an artist. She learned to accept the negatives and revel in the positives.

He encouraged her to experiment with different media and new subjects, and the world cracked open, revealing its secrets: the magic in broken bottles, the beauty in weathered brick. She carried a sketchpad everywhere—on the bus, in math class. Once, when she was at lunch with friends, she snuck off to the bathroom to sketch something on a napkin, wondering if this was how addicts felt. Her confidence grew, and she dared to see herself as a talented artist. It was a heady feeling.

When Fletcher asked her if she'd gotten any ideas from visiting the Mütter, she lied and said no, though she'd been back several times. She wanted to surprise him with her final term project even before it was due. It was a painting of hundreds of tiny conjoined twins, arranged in patterns to form an image that could only be seen from a distance: two girls holding hands in a field of wildflowers. She called it "DNA."

She put the finishing touches on the project a week before it was due and couldn't wait to show him, even though it wasn't their usual meeting day. She made her way to the art studio at the end of the day, clutching her portfolio to her chest and doing her best to avoid colliding with the hordes of students headed toward the doors. The studio was deserted, so she went downstairs to his office. She knocked on his door and announced herself, the sound of her voice echoing down the empty hall.

"Come in." Fletcher looked up from his desk. "I wasn't expecting you."

"I want to show you my project," she said in a little-girl voice she couldn't control. Her hands shook as she unzipped her portfolio case. It was judgment day, and her piece was so much more than a painting. It was a statement of her creative vision and of her close and complex relationship with her sister.

She turned and propped the canvas up on a table, leaning it against the wall. Standing close, you could see the hundreds of tiny figures she'd spent weeks drawing, their bodies entwined. Helena stepped back, and the twin girls reappeared. "You have to stand back to see the big picture," she said.

A low voice came from somewhere. "You're so good." Were the twins speaking to her? *Yes, tell me I'm good*, she said to the girls and closed her eyes. Their hands were on her shoulders, feathery breath on her face.

But it was *his* breath, *his* hands forcing her against the wall. Helena stared over his shoulder at a room that was coming undone, shifting and reconnecting at odd angles, until there was nothing solid left except the hard wall against her back, the grinding of his body against hers. She pushed against him, but he was too strong for her. "No," she yelled as he grabbed the elastic waistband of her slacks and underpants and pulled them both down. She tried to push his arms away, but her hands were pinned against his chest. "No," she repeated again and again. His fingers probed her, and he whispered, "You're so beautiful. I have to. You…" He invaded her mouth with his tongue as he unzipped his jeans. He tasted like garlic. She gagged. If she could throw up, he might let her go. But he pressed his body so tightly against her she couldn't move, she couldn't turn, she couldn't vomit, she couldn't utter a sound because her throat and vocal chords had shut down. She was the Soap Lady, her useless mouth a gaping hole. *Remarkably, the body maintains both its overall shape and appearance.* Then the friction of skin on skin. Then pressure, then pain, then…nothing.

When it was over, he turned away, still breathing heavily. She fastened her pants with trembling fingers, picked up her canvas, and walked out into the empty hall. In the girls' room she cleaned herself up as best she could. If she ran into anyone who noticed the blood, she'd let them assume it was her period, not the stain of his violation.

Somehow, she made it home, still shaking, with no memory of the walk from school, and slipped unnoticed into her room. She stripped off the pants and sweater she was wearing and put on a ratty T-shirt and sweatpants. Claiming an upset stomach, she skipped dinner and played back what had happened that afternoon in an endless loop. Had she been complicit in the act? He said, *I have to. You...* You what? You made me do this? Why would he be any different from the other guys who looked at her like that? Wasn't it her responsibility to keep her looks under wrap? She stood slouching in front of the mirror. What if I'd been wearing this? Would he have raped me in this? Maybe...probably. A burst of anger stiffened her back. Do they expect me to wear a fucking burqa?

He'd seen her vulnerability and taken advantage of it. She picked up a tube of lipstick and drew the outline of a dog on the mirror. That's what he saw—a cute little mutt. *She looks hungry. I think I'll feed her. Bet she'll eat out of my hand. Bet she'll roll over if I pet her.* Helena stared at the lipstick dog with the shaggy hair that looked like Fletcher's hair. *No, he's the dog.* She wet a washcloth with shampoo and worked on the mirror. The lipstick was greasy and didn't want to come off, so she rubbed harder. *Getting me drunk on false praise, talking to me like I was Michael-fucking-Angelo, screwing with me.* Her hand ached. She wanted to shred the sketches, slash the painting, destroy everything he'd polluted with his lying green pen. Then the violation would be complete.

Instead, she stashed her "DNA" canvas at the back of the closet. Then she gathered her art supplies, sketchbooks, and paintings and shoved them in as well. Now what? Call the police? That's probably what Jenna would tell her to do—the smart thing to do. But it was too late, wasn't it? She'd already taken a long, hot shower. Stupid. She'd destroyed the "evidence." No one had seen it happen. It would be "he said, she said" — and "he said" trumped "she said" every time. She wasn't even sure her parents would believe her. And what good would come from her publicly accusing him? She could be saving another girl from the same fate. Would Fletcher be fired even if they didn't believe her? No. And she'd be...exposed. She curled up tight like a conch shell on top of the covers, making herself as small as she could, and thought about taking another shower.

Helena stayed home the next day and the day after that, claiming she had a fever and it felt like the flu. There were only three weeks till the end of the school year, so she could feign a mysterious illness like chronic fatigue syndrome and miss the rest of the year. Her parents would be all over her, but she'd never tell them the real reason for her absence.

As it turned out, her parents were so immersed in their professional lives—her father with his medical practice, her mother with the academics and politics of higher education—that they didn't notice the change in her behavior and believed her when she said she had the flu. But she didn't fool her sister. Helena was not one to miss two days of school.

That night, Jenna knocked on Helena's bedroom door.

"Come in." Helena's voice was soft and gravelly.

Jenna stood at the door, her head tilted. "You don't really have the flu, do you?"

Helena could have protested, but she knew her expression would give her away. She wore her emotions like clown make-up, no matter how hard she tried to hide them. She sat up and clutched the covers to her chest like a floral shield, her long black hair accentuating the pallor of her face. "I'm sick, but not that way."

Jenna's eyes narrowed with concern. She sat on the edge of the bed and put her hand on Helena's shoulder.

"I'm..." Tears filled Helena's eyes.

Jenna stroked her sister's shoulder. "Take your time, Lena."

"Oh, Jen. I'm broken." Helena sobbed. It was the first time she'd cried since the attack, and now she was afraid she wouldn't be able to stop. "I...he..." She wiped her eyes with the sheet but continued sobbing. "He raped me." The words stung like acid on her tongue.

"He? Who? No, don't say anything yet." She wrapped her arms around her sister, and the two hugged for a long time. A car door slammed, and the grandfather clock downstairs struck nine.

Helena took a deep breath, inhaling the familiar citrusy

smell of Jenna's freshly shampooed hair, and whispered, "Fletcher."

Jenna shuddered, and for a moment it felt to Helena like she was the one comforting her sister. When they finally pulled apart, Helena told Jenna what had happened and watched her words translate into shock that played on her sister's face, as if she, too, were living the experience. Jenna advised her to report the incident to the police and the school administration, but Helena told her she dreaded the publicity and the gossip—saying it would feel like being attacked all over again.

"Well, if it happened to me, I'd report him," said Jenna. "At least I think I would. You might be right that the blowback would be worse for you than for him. But..." She waited so long, Helena wondered if she'd forgotten what she was going to say. "But if you don't say anything, he might do it again."

Helena put her hand to her mouth and looked out the window at the neighbor's lights peeking through the trees. Then she lowered her hand and turned back to Jenna. "I don't think he's going to do anything like that again. He's been at the school for a long time, and there haven't been any rumors. And...this is going to sound crazy, like I'm full of myself or something, but I think it happened because of me."

"Lena. Don't *ever* say that."

"That came out wrong. I'm not blaming myself. What I mean is he saw me as this vulnerable person, hungry for affirmation. Maybe vulnerability was a trigger."

"And you're beautiful, even when you slump down and cover yourself in baggy clothes. But you're not the only attractive, insecure girl at school. What's to stop him from—"

"I don't think he will. I think something weird was going on with us, but I didn't read the signals."

"So, you *are* blaming yourself?"

"N-no." Helena stuttered. Then she inhaled sharply and repeated, "No," in a firm, confident voice. "Never." Though there had been a moment the night before when she thought she'd been complicit, her anger at Fletcher had snuffed out that thought.

"Do you want me to take you to a doctor? Get...you know... checked out."

"No. I'm okay. And please don't tell Mom and Dad."

"Because?"

"Because I'd rather keep it between the two of us. And I'm thinking of finishing out the school year. I'm not going to let him screw up the end of my junior year—make me miss finals."

"But what if you see him?"

"I'll make sure I don't," she said with more confidence than she felt. "And I'll bet he'll do his darndest to avoid me." The corners of her mouth turned up. "He might even be afraid of me. Imagine that."

The last three weeks of school felt like three years. Helena avoided the art wing, and the one time she spotted Fletcher talking to a student in the hall, she hurried off in the other direction, her heart pounding. She wondered if he was being equally vigilant in avoiding her.

When a girl in her art class asked why she hadn't been to class, Helena told her she was working on an independent project.

"You could cut class and you'd still get an A," said the girl, "because you're the teacher's pet."

Helena's face burned as she remembered the lipstick dog she'd drawn on the mirror. But the girl had been right about the A. In addition to that, Fletcher mailed her a glowing college recommendation in advance of the college applications she'd be submitting in the fall. Her first instinct was to rip it up, but why should she punish herself?

The only time she allowed herself to relax was at lunch with Jenna and Elliot. The three of them ate every day at a small table in the far corner of the cafeteria. The first time Elliot sat across from Helena after the rape, he ran a hand through his thick brown hair, lowered his heavy eyebrows, and remarked, "There's something wrong. What's up?"

"I'm not ready to talk about it yet, but thanks for asking."

She had no intention of telling him, but that was about to change. The week after school ended, she missed her period. She bought three pregnancy test kits and locked herself in the bathroom. The first strip turned pink. Could have been a false positive. Same result with the next two. Distraught, she shoved the kits into the plastic bag from the drugstore to dispose of later in secret.

Back in her bedroom, she covered her head with a pillow and cried silently until there were no tears left. Then, dry-eyed, she pulled one of her sketchpads out of the closet and ripped a page out through the spiral coils, crumpled it, and threw it into the corner. Then she tore out another page and did the same. She ripped out the third page and was about to discard that one as well when she looked at what she'd sketched: a detailed rendering of the conjoined twins. She propped it up against some books on her bookshelf. The next few pages were different iterations of the twins, and she propped them up as well. There were other sketches of disjointed limbs, distorted skulls, the skeleton of a dwarf next to that of a giant. All freaks. She stuck them up on her walls with removable tape and went back to ripping out pages.

"What are you doing in there?" Jenna called out on the other side of the door. "Sounds like you're driving a car over railroad tracks."

"I'm ripping out my sketches." Helena's voice broke.

"You're not really—"

Helena tore out another page, and Jenna burst into the room.

"Don't rip up your drawings."

"Ripping *out,* not *up.*"

Jenna's eyes widened at the sight of the sketches papering the walls. "What's all this?"

"Freaks." Helena was holding a sketch of deformed fetuses floating in jars of liquid. She sank to the floor, and Jenna sat down next to her. They sat quietly, shoulder to shoulder, as if conjoined. Jenna, who had never been a hugger, put her arms around her sister. The gesture loosened something inside Helena. "I'm pregnant."

"Oh, Lena."

They sat in silence for a while.

"What do you want to do?"

Elliot drove to the clinic while the two sisters sat in back. Helena felt nothing but the need to rid herself of the thing growing inside her—a thing that was freaky like Fletcher, like her, like the fetuses in those glass cases with their missing craniums, fused limbs, cyclops eyes. Thank God she lived in a state where they didn't make you wait seventy-two hours, force you to get an ultrasound, or ask you what Jesus would do.

Jenna held her hand until they took her into the operating room. Her brain was as numb as the part they anesthetized, as numb as she'd been after Fletcher impregnated her. Afterward she rested in the recovery room, where Jenna was a silent presence, gently rubbing her arm and shoulder. When she was able to stand, Jenna guided her to the car.

It was only when they were back on the road that Jenna said, "You must have been so scared."

"No, Jen. I felt nothing."

Their parents were away at a medical conference, so the house was empty. Upstairs, Helena pulled a pair of baggy sweatpants and an oversized T-shirt out of her dresser drawer and changed in the bathroom. When she slipped under the dusty rose floral quilt on her bed, she noticed her sister standing in the corner, watching her.

"What?"

"Want me to stay with you? I can sleep in the other bed. Like when we were kids."

"No, I'm okay. I just want to sleep.

"Can I ask you a really personal question? You're going to think I'm weird."

"Nah. Nothing you could ask me at this point would embarrass me." She closed her eyes.

"Okay. What was it like...the other thing?"

"What other thing?"

"To have a man want you like that. I don't mean the physical...you know...the deed. I mean the wanting."

Helena opened her eyes. "The what?"

"The way he wanted you."

The question shocked her. Didn't her sister get it? "He raped me, for God's sake," she said angrily.

"I know. It must have been hell for you. It's just...I don't know if anyone will ever want me like that."

Yes, someone will love you someday, Helena wanted to answer, but her eyelids were so heavy, her jaw slack.

She heard the bedroom door shut, and before she drifted off, she thought, Yes, someone will love you, but I'm not sure that's in the cards for me.

The freaks stayed on the walls for a month. Helena felt like one of them. She had lost the desire to draw or paint, and her materials stayed in the closet. As time passed, she felt increasingly adrift. She missed the joy of her craft. So, one day in early August, she took down the drawings and stashed them in a drawer. Then she retrieved her pencils, acrylics, brushes, and sketchbooks from the closet and set up an easel in the corner of the room. Throughout the rest of the summer, the act of filling her sketchbooks became a source of strength, and she began to think of herself as a survivor, despite her anxiety about the coming school year and the possibility of running into Fletcher.

She needn't have worried. Fletcher didn't return in the fall. Students made all kinds of speculations as to why he left, but the general consensus was that he got a better job somewhere else. Helena did an independent study with the teacher who replaced him. After a couple of months working together, he gave her an excellent recommendation. Helena was accepted everywhere she applied. She hadn't needed Fletcher's approval after all; her art spoke for itself. She and Jenna took great pleasure in burning his letter of recommendation in the backyard.

Helena ended up at the Tyler School of Art in Philadelphia, where she mostly kept to herself. Her feeling of empowerment flagged as men continued to hit on her, and she found herself slouching again.

Then she met Matt when they were both seniors. On the first day of photography class, they met in the darkroom, where he was watching her develop a print.

"You're a natural," he said.

"Last time I heard that was eleventh grade."

Much later, after she'd moved in with him, she told him about Fletcher. They were lying in bed, and first he turned out the bedroom lamp. She couldn't imagine the story would change his feelings about her; she just didn't want to see the shock, pity, or other emotions that might play out on his face when she told him. He smoothed her hair as she talked. Then she turned on the light, wanting to see him after all, and his dark eyes were filled with tears, as were hers.

"Besides Jenna and Elliot, you're the only one who knows."

Matt took her hand. "Thank you for trusting me." Matt looked so much like her that when they went out to dinner with Jenna and her fiancé, people often mistook the two of them for brother and sister.

They lay together in silence. Someone coughed in the apartment next door. The water pipes vibrated as someone turned off a tap.

"He complimented my work for months," Helena said, "and I took it at face value. I think he was just playing with me."

"You think so? Your early work was exceptional. How could he not have been impressed?"

"Maybe he was. But he'd gotten a good look at me before he saw my work, and I think that impressed him even more. After that, I never felt safe with a man until I met you. I trusted you from the beginning."

"Why's that?"

She hesitated a moment before responding. "Because we met in a dark room. You couldn't see me, so you got to know me from the inside out."

Matt laughed, and they turned off the light.

The baby kicked again. Helena checked her watch. She'd been standing across the street from the Mütter for half an hour, and she had only a few minutes to walk five blocks to meet Matt at their favorite Thai restaurant. Still she lingered. Helena remembered the display case of deformed fetuses in jars and wondered what the clinic had done with her own baby: Had they flushed it down the toilet, or dumped it into a biohazard bag? Had it been a boy or a girl?

For eight months, she'd done everything the books had told her—organic baby clothes and bedding, lots of Mozart, no soft cheeses. At her last ultrasound, the doctor told her everything seemed perfect. She knew her daughter wouldn't be perfect.

Matt, a computer graphics designer, once told her that he built software updates into the existing functionality of an app, fixing flaws and adding new features to create the best version of the software for the time being. Future updates would bring the software closer to the designer's vision, but a good app was always a work in progress. Helena would do her best to teach her daughter about vulnerability and resilience and empowerment; the rest would be up to her.

Helena remembered another display she'd seen on her many visits to the museum: the model of a full-term fetus curled in a thick oval shell, which was painted on the outside like a Ukrainian Easter egg. That's how she liked to picture her daughter. A Matryoshka doll, layered with unlimited possibilities.

The late afternoon sun was low in the sky, casting a warm, golden glow on the museum. Helena pulled out her cell phone and took a photo as inspiration for a future painting. Then she straightened her shoulders and walked to the restaurant to meet her husband.

Beautocracy

Pamela put on her long black wig, stepped into a pair of stilettos, and headed for her job interview at the high school. *I'm a damn good teacher,* she thought. *They'd be idiots not to offer me the position.* But when she stepped into the office and the principal greeted her with pursed lips and narrowed eyes, she knew the deck was stacked against her, despite the resumé that had gotten her in the door.

The principal was petite, with blond hair and a kewpie-doll face. "I'm sorry, but there's no need to go on with an interview," she told Pamela.

"You mean my Ph.D. and references count for nothing?"

"That's not what I'm saying. But we have to weigh all the factors. Students learn more from attractive teachers than unattractive ones. The research is indisputable."

The kewpie-doll principal tapped her leg impatiently, but Pamela was not one to give in easily. She pulled a batch of student testimonials out of her briefcase.

"When you weigh all the factors, shouldn't you take past performance into account?" She handed the packet over to the interviewer, who glanced at the top sheet and handed it back.

"Very nice," she said condescendingly, "but we've inter-viewed several other candidates with Ph.D.s and rave reviews. And all other things being equal..."

All other things were *not* equal. Since the Supreme Court had ruled that companies could use physical attractiveness as a consideration in their hiring practices, studies suddenly con-firmed the so-called "beauty premium," showing that beautiful people brought in more money for their employers, were more productive, received higher salaries, and were more intelli-gent than their less attractive counterparts. Never mind who'd funded them.

At thirty-one, Pamela didn't need to be reminded by the principal of her physical shortcomings. There were official tools to do that for her. She had uploaded her most flattering photo to an attractiveness calculator app. The app compared her features to the template of the perfect face as defined by the Golden Ratio, a configuration that occurs repeatedly in nature and art and is considered universally pleasing to the eye.

Pamela had followed the instructions on the screen to mark the contours of her face; she moved yellow arrows to the out-side edges of her right and left eyes, a red line to the bottom of her chin, blue lines to the right and left sides of her nose, until she'd marked the position of every feature. Then she clicked Submit. Earlier versions of these calculators had been accompanied by warnings, the gist being, *If you have issues of low esteem and lack of confidence, do not take this test.* Nowadays, wom-en were urged to use the tool as a starting point on the path to perfection. Even the president had weighed in, saying, "You're responsible for the way you look. If you haven't done every-thing to make yourself beautiful, it's your own damn fault."

The calculator had rendered its judgment in searing red let-ters: *You are ugly!* On a scale of one to ten, she'd scored a two—just one notch above "very ugly." The score was accompanied by a long list of specifics, but she stopped reading after the first six:

Poor facial symmetry

Poor face shape
Eyes set too close
Mouth too small for nose
Nose too wide
Chin OK

The words on the screen were like a judgment from the Almighty, a final grade of F on her permanent record.

Women using the site could also get a picture of themselves after "corrective" surgery, with an automatic referral to the cosmetic surgeon sponsoring the website. They were just a nip and tuck away from going to sleep a *two* and waking up a *nine* or *ten*. And all of it was covered by insurance. No copays, no deductibles. Perfection on the cheap.

Many women she knew had already gone under the knife, and the rest seemed to be making plans. But not Pamela. She and her sister, Alice, had sworn to each other that they'd never give in to the "beautocracy," a term Pamela had coined in her dissertation. Alice liked to say that their oyster-shell exteriors were protective covers for the pearls hidden inside.

Attractiveness had always been a valued commodity. But now women were paying a penalty for not living up to the new expectations. It was becoming harder—often dangerous—for women who looked like Pamela to walk the streets. Which is why she had worn stilettos and covered her frizzy hair with a wig for this interview.

Pamela's two best features—great legs and a photogenic smile—didn't move the principal. She simply stood and crossed her arms, effectively ending the interview.

Pamela stuffed the folder back into her briefcase. When she stood, she was several inches taller than the little kewpie, which gave her a fleeting sense of superiority. She strode to the door and then stopped. "Your loss. I have more to offer than a dozen air-headed...Oh, hell. Never mind." She slammed the door behind her.

Fueled by anger and frustration, Pamela strode briskly toward the bus stop, brushing past women with gauze wound around their necks, stretched over chins and foreheads, women wearing their bandages as casually as accessories. She barely missed bumping into a woman who had stopped to admire herself in a store window and was gazing down at her chest in awe, as if her enhanced breasts were shiny new toys. *The female body as playground.*

Pamela stopped short when she spotted two men in identical black leather jackets up ahead. The monster-face insignias embossed on their jackets and the black leather boots and aviator glasses identified them as self-styled "streetcleaners" on the prowl for "beasties." That was the new catchword for women like her. Pamela turned and race-walked in the opposite direction, her high heels tack-tacking against the pavement. Damned stilettos had become a de facto fashion standard, and anyone wearing heels lower than three inches faced ridicule—or worse. She needed high heels to maintain a low profile.

Pamela was breathing hard by the time she caught up with a group of young girls, their heads buried in their electronic devices as they walked, except when they looked up to communicate with each other. Their long, silky hair bounced as they strode confidently in their high heels, some wearing bandages. They couldn't have been over fifteen. According to the new conventional wisdom, it was never too early to get started on the road to perfection. Pamela followed close behind on the chance that someone in the crowd might come to her aid if the vigilantes decided to rough her up. Not likely. People had become less tolerant of beasties once plastic surgery had become free. *If you're still a beastie, it's your own damn fault.* She took a quick look behind her. No leather jackets in sight.

Pamela's anger was still burning white hot when she got to her apartment, so she called her sister. Alice had been the youngest member of the House of Representatives until being voted out in the last election. She'd been enormously popular—a passionate advocate for her constituents and a tireless spokesperson for women's rights—until the beauty cult got a stranglehold on the neck of the American public. Pamela had watched the televised debate, cringing when Alice's opponent pointed a finger and said, "Look at her. Why would anyone vote for someone with a face like that?" A majority of her constituents apparently agreed, because she lost the election.

"What are you planning to do, now that you can't teach?" Alice asked.

"Beats me." Pamela paused. "I'm sure I'll find something. Otherwise I'll have to leave Philly." Silence.

"I'm not sure I can stay in Virginia, either."

"Where would you go?

"Oregon," said Alice. She explained how she was working with a group of fellow activists to set up a sanctuary city in Portland for women like them. It was going to take a few months to get everything set up; then Pamela could join her.

"That sounds promising. I'll find something for now," said Pamela. They said goodbye. It wouldn't be easy for her to find work; companies were demanding beauty for everything, even research positions and back office jobs, claiming that the presence of unattractive women had a negative effect on morale.

Pamela took out the family photo album to remind herself why she stayed the course. Paging through the gallery of black-and-whites, Kodacolors, and Polaroids going back four generations, she was once again struck by the family resemblance—the close-set eyes, the large nose. None of the women in her family had been conventionally attractive, but the intelligence and determination that shone through those less-than-perfectly-spaced eyes projected all the beauty that mattered. Pamela was descended from a line of fighters, from Alice Paul to her grandmother and mother. All had been leaders in the women's movement. Adopting a new face would be a betrayal. And as a student of history and sociology, Pamela knew the importance of continuity and the price one paid for tearing down the past.

Eventually Pamela found work as a part-time fact-checker. It was an online gig that barely paid the rent, even for her cheap, third-floor walkup in a down-at-the-heels townhouse complex in Northeast Philadelphia. But if she could just hang in for a few more months, she'd be able to leave Philly and join the resistance. The movement seemed to be growing, albeit slowly. There were stories of brave women who spoke out at the risk of public humiliation, planned strategies to confront Congress, and established safe houses around the country. The resisters called themselves WYSIWYG (What You See Is What You Get), pronounced "wizzywig."

Pamela usually did her shopping online, to avoid going into the street. But one evening she ran out of tampons, and her period was heavy. She needed to go to the pharmacy. So, after finishing her day's assignment, she put on her wig and high heels as the TV droned in the background. Something about the streetcleaners being granted official status under the umbrella of the Department of Health and Human Services. To her, they were still goon squads, and she hoped she wouldn't encounter any on her way to the pharmacy.

Bewigged and dressed in a heavy coat and scarf, she made her way carefully along snow-covered sidewalks to the pharmacy, her pace slowed by her stiletto boots. Once inside, she made sure no one else was in the aisle she needed before venturing down it. Besides the cashier and the pharmacist, she appeared to be the only one there.

Pamela located the tampons at the end of an aisle stocked with contraceptives, erectile dysfunction drugs, and morning-after pills. After the president had been overheard saying, "We'd all be safer if every man could get laid on a regular basis (hey, I was only joking)," researchers released studies that identified sexual frustration as a primary cause of violence. After that, Congress voted to make both Viagra and birth control available over the counter. Who said Congress didn't believe in science? Then they'd legalized prostitution and, after considerable debate, voted to make abortion legal, for registered prostitutes that is, all for the sake of national security and economic growth.

The heat in the store was cranked up to equatorial levels, so she unzipped her overcoat and unwrapped the scarf that covered the lower half of her face. She passed the cosmetics aisle on the way to the cashier, and as she reached down for a tube of lipstick, she caught the movement of a dark figure out of the corner of her eye—a man in a black leather jacket, gloves, boots, and black knit cap. Maybe he'd turn at the cross aisle. No such luck; he was headed toward her.

The scent of exotic perfumes in the next aisle hung heavy as tropical vines, sweat trickled down her neck and between her breasts, and her heart pounded a jungle beat. Now the stranger was standing next to her. He raised his gloved hand, and Pamela braced for a slap, a shove, a grab. Instead, he pulled off his hat, releasing a cascade of blond hair. Not a he. A she. Pamela's relief was tempered by the thought that women could sometimes be as cruel as men.

"Damn, it's hot in here," said the blonde.

Unable to speak, Pamela nodded.

"Know where the tampons are?"

Pamela giggled at the unexpected question. "Over there." She giggled again.

The blonde gave her a puzzled look, shook her head slowly, and walked away.

Pamela paid and walked outside. Though her escape to Portland was months away, the possibility of a brighter future lightened her step. She stood tall, taking long, confident strides, remembering how it felt to be normal. Until she heard the voice behind her.

"Think you're hot stuff strutting like a model, Beastie?"

The voice was male but high-pitched, like the voice of an adolescent on the cusp of manhood. She couldn't see his face as he encircled her waist from behind with one leather-clad arm and covered her mouth with his other hand, cutting her off mid-scream. Pamela tried to shake herself free but couldn't loosen his vise-like grip. Definitely not an adolescent.

Her assailant dragged her down the deserted sidewalk to a narrow alley between two blocks of brick townhouses. The alley was dark, the only light coming from a couple of windows on either side. Overflowing trash cans saturated the air with the stench of rotting garbage. Her attacker jerked her around and slammed her against the rough brick wall.

Pamela tried to grab the lid of a metal trash can to defend herself, but it slipped from her grasp, hitting the ground like a cymbal, the sound playing encores between the buildings. Startled, her assailant lifted his hand from her mouth, and she screamed.

"Do that again, Beastie, and I'll kill you," he said. The light from an overhead window cast shadows on a sharp-featured, ferret-like face distorted by rage. He pressed the point of a knife against her throat, and she froze. With his free hand, he unzipped her jacket.

"Damn, Beastie," he said, gripping one of her breasts through the thin material of her T-shirt. "Nothing to hold on to." She screamed again, and he pressed the knife deeper into her neck. She was pretty sure he was drawing blood. "I'll teach you to go out looking like this."

A window above them opened, and a man yelled, "What the hell's goin' on down there? Get off my property, or I'll call the cops."

"Help!" she screamed, but the man had already slammed the window shut.

Her attacker fumbled to lower the zipper of his jeans, cursing when it got stuck. The guy was at least a foot taller than she was and built like a linebacker. His unlikely soprano voice would have provided comic relief under other circumstances. She was tempted to insult his manhood, but he'd undoubtedly finish the job on her neck if she did. His zipper was down, and he was reaching inside his pants when a police siren rang out, ear-splittingly loud, as if the car were right there in the alley. Her attacker froze and then laughed when the theme song of a well-known police procedural followed the siren. The sound was coming through an open window above them.

The guy will probably kill me after he...after he...Stop! No way this rodent-faced shit is going to rape me. But she didn't have a weapon. Or did she? Stiletto boots! She was wearing her weapons. Pamela had taken self-defense classes. She'd practiced disabling mock assailants by jamming a high heel into the top of a foot.

Mustering all her energy, she rammed a stiletto heel into his foot, and he let out a banshee scream. As he pulled the knife from her neck and began to bend over to nurse his injured foot, she jammed a knee into his crotch for good measure. Then she ran down the alley, setting trash cans clattering like angry timpani. Her heel hit something slippery, but she managed to stay upright. She risked a quick look behind her. The would-be rapist was still tending to his injured parts. She pulled off her boots and ran in stocking feet. The initial shock of the snow was soon replaced by numbness, as if she were running on wooden blocks. Somehow, she was able to make it home.

Pamela sat on the edge of the tub and ran warm water over her feet until the feeling returned. She then filled the tub with hot water and got in. She closed her eyes and imagined what would happen if she went to the police, took her attacker to court, and made him pay. But she knew how that would play out. They'd laugh at her and insist it couldn't have happened because she was so coyote ugly that no one would want to rape the likes of her. For all she knew, "coyote ugly" was now a legitimate defense for rapists. She hoped that wouldn't be the case in Portland.

On the day of her departure, Pamela swathed her head in gauze, texted her sister, and left a voicemail message. She hadn't been able to contact Alice for the last couple of days, but since they'd already firmed up the date and time of her arrival, there was really no need. Pamela called a car service to take her to Thirtieth Street Station, where she'd hop a train to the airport. Then she rolled her suitcase into the hallway and closed her apartment door for the last time.

When the car turned off I-95 and headed across town, Pamela bade silent goodbyes to the landmarks that had been fixtures in her life—Independence Hall, the Academy of Music. Her heart zigzagged in her chest when they stopped for a red light in front of the new Franklin Clinic. Once they moved past, she breathed easier, knowing her journey wouldn't end there. She couldn't bear to think about what they did to women in places like that.

Thirtieth Street Station, a neoclassical style building dominated by massive Corinthian columns, was her gateway to freedom. The exterior was off-putting—made of huge marble blocks, turned gray by age and pollution. But the interior was welcoming despite the presence of goon squads and crowds of people. There was something almost spiritual about the warm light filtering through cathedral-like windows, the travel announcements echoing as incomprehensibly as murmured prayers, the art deco chandeliers hanging like giant paper lanterns from an intricately patterned ceiling. Lost in a sea of fellow travelers, many of them sporting bandages like hers, she pictured the trains beneath them, carrying passengers in all directions, carrying her to freedom. What was it about this place that felt so welcoming? Then she realized. The building was a metaphor for her situation. Its off-putting façade hid a beautiful interior. The pearl in the oyster shell.

When she got to the airport, Pamela texted her sister and called again. Still no answer. But she was too excited to worry, and when the plane took off, Pamela's heart soared in tandem. Only a few more hours, and she'd be reunited with her sister. Her twin sister. Her mirror image. The two would act with one mind, as they always had, and keep feminism alive, following in the footsteps of the family matriarchs. Pamela turned her head toward the window and put on a sleep mask. In spite of the media's blind eye and the president's proposal to impose sanctions on sanctuary cities, she imagined the resistance movement steadily growing, supported by a small but vocal network of churches. When Pamela finally dozed, lulled by the steady drone of the engines, she dreamed of a massive choir of resisters singing Handel's "Hallelujah" chorus at Thirtieth Street Station.

Security at Portland International was tight. When a guard questioned her, scrutinizing her face and her ID to make sure they matched, she responded with a laugh. "Looks like I need a new ID." He smiled and let her go, but as she walked to the ground transportation counter, she looked back and saw him pick up his cell phone. *Don't be paranoid. Three-quarters of the people at this airport are on cell phones at this very moment.*

After arranging for a car, Pamela went outside to wait. When the driver signaled her to get in, she gave him her sister's address and got into the back seat. *So close! What a relief.* She closed her eyes and drifted off. When she awakened with a start, she checked the time. Twenty minutes had elapsed. Her sister lived close to the airport. Why was the ride taking so long? And now they were driving down city streets. Her sister lived in the 'burbs. This wasn't right.

"Stop the car," she said. "Let me out."

The driver didn't turn around. When they stopped for a red light, she tried the door, but it was locked.

"Let me out," she screamed. No response.

They pulled up to a sprawling, glass-clad building, and the driver cut the engine. The sign over the door read Portland Rejuvenation Clinic. Two leather-jacketed goons opened the door, locked arms with her, and walked her inside. She thought fleetingly of her luggage; it hardly mattered. One of the goons stayed with her as they checked her in, a process that took a while because she struggled. They had to press her index finger to the scanner three times before it registered her fingerprint. The woman at the desk didn't appear the least bit concerned.

Under the watchful eyes of the goon, Pamela sat in one of the few empty chairs in a large waiting room. Except for a couple of anxious faces, the women filling the room appeared happy to be there. The blue-gray walls were dotted with portraits of women with perfect faces. Other than differences in skin tone and hair color, they looked pretty much alike. A plaque on the wall read *Ask at the desk to see the "before" photos.*

Alice *had* to get her out of there. Pamela reached for her cell phone. *Calm down.* She took a deep breath and quickly scanned the room. No one was looking at her. With shaking hands, she pressed her sister's number. *Please pick up.* She heard the familiar voicemail greeting and waited for the beep. Damn. "*Please,* Allie, pick up," she whispered. "They've taken me to a clinic downtown. They're going to—"

Her sister's voice broke in. "Oh, Pammy. I'm so sorry. I didn't mean for this to happen. Hang in there. I'll be there." Thank God. Her sister would take care of her.

A statuesque woman in a tight white uniform towered over her. "Don't worry, dear. Everything's going to be okay. Just a few forms to fill out." She handed Pamela a tablet. "Bring it to the front desk when you're done, and I'll escort you in."

Was this the form that let women opt out? The Supreme Court had ruled that what she was about to undergo was legal, but it was unconstitutional to force women to do this surgery without their consent. So, they'd come up with a workaround: A women could refuse "treatment," but she'd be charged an opt-out fee steep enough to bankrupt all but the super-rich. But the online forms in front of her were strictly medical. Apparently, opting out was no longer an option.

Still, Pamela breathed a little easier, knowing her sister was on her way. Allie would save her. Get her out before they strapped her to a bed, anesthetized her, and carved her a new face and body; before they did a pregnancy test and, if the result was positive, performed an abortion; before they tied her tubes, since there was a high probability that the offspring of a beastie would be another beastie, no matter how much exterior work they did on the mother; before she woke up a stranger, with a set of new breasts, a face that was no longer her own, and no chance of having a child.

A handsome male doctor came to fetch her. The clinic was set up like a hospital emergency department, with curtained rooms surrounding a central station. The doctor led her into one of the rooms and strapped her to the bed with leather restraints as she struggled against them. "I'm sorry," he said, "but you know how this works."

"No," she cried, her wrists chafing against the leather. "No, please." But he was gone. "Please," she whimpered to the empty room. She looked around at the machines, the boxes of bandages and metal objects that would be used to carve her up.

She was alone, with only photographs of beautiful women to keep her company. The sign above them read *One of these can be you.* A collection of baby pictures hung on a side wall under a sign that read *One of these can be yours.* Adoption was available for ex-beasties who wanted children. A paternalistic Congress had ruled that motherhood was a sacred right and should be available to all women, even beasties. Sterilized women could choose from a catalogue of naturally beautiful surrogates impregnated with the sperm of carefully selected men. Surrogates and sperm donors were paid big bucks to produce smart, beautiful children so that beasties could be granted the privilege of motherhood.

The hum of activity on the other side of the curtain was broken by the occasional raised voice and the periodic click-click of stilettos against tile. *Please, Allie, hurry!*

A nurse pulled the curtain. "This'll calm you down, honey." The nurse's shrill voice was as reassuring as metal on metal. She jabbed a needle in Pamela's arm. As a drug-induced warmth suffused her body, Pamela heard her sister's voice in the hall.

"Allie," she cried, but it came out a hoarse whisper. The curtain opened, and a woman walked in. A woman with long legs, sleek black hair, and perfect features. A nurse? Something about the eyes gave Pamela a strange feeling. Then the stranger spoke. It was her sister's voice—the voice she knew as well as her own. Her sister's voice, coming from that alien body.

"I'm so sorry, Pamela. I wanted to tell you before you got here, but I didn't have the heart. I fought with everything I had, but people refused to listen. They were put off by my looks."

Our looks.

"No one believes anything coming from the mouth of a beastie anymore. So—"

Pamela's mind was fuzzy. Could she be hallucinating? No, this was real. It took all her energy to form the question, "Did they...make you...do it?"

Her sister's eyes were dissolving in sorrow. "No, nobody forced me. I just realized I could accomplish more if I...tweaked my exterior. They even promised me a job as a legislative aide for a state senator if I fixed myself up. They said I'd be in a better position to advocate for women's rights as an insider rather than an outsider. And you can help me, after you—"

"But I don't want to..." Pamela tried to fight the sedating effects of the drug, but it was no use. A tear traced a path down her cheek, a mirror image of the tear she saw running down her sister's face, before it shimmered, blurred, and disappeared.

Acknowledgments

I couldn't have gotten this far on my journey without the help and encouragement of so many people.

First, I'd like to thank my tenth grade English teacher, Mr. Mims. Though he didn't remember me when I contacted him recently, I will never forget his positive feedback and the confidence it instilled in me. I'd also like to thank Barry Dinerman, my first creative writing teacher and mentor, without whom I would never have attempted to write fiction. Barry encouraged me, coached me in the basics of good writing, and taught me that every single word counts in a short story. Thanks also to Phyllis Mass, an instructor at Temple University's lifelong learning program, whose improvisational writing techniques helped me get the words to flow when my brain wouldn't cooperate.

Heartfelt thanks to my colleagues at the Buck County Writing Workshop and its intrepid leader, Don Swaim. Their writing has inspired me, and their critiques have been invaluable in helping me hone my craft.

Thanks also to my editor, the brilliant Janet Benton, who helped me dig deeper into my characters and fill in all the missing pieces. And to Di Freeze who dotted Is, crossed Ts, did the layout, and shepherded this book through production.

Finally, a special note of love and gratitude for my husband, Jim, an eagled-eyed proofreader, who patiently let me "do my thing," and who almost always stopped talking to me when I was writing.

Made in the USA
Lexington, KY
27 September 2019